Readers love the Iron Eagle Gym series by SEAN MICHAEL

The New Boy

"This is classic Sean Michael and a fun story that is quick and easy to read."

—Prism Book Alliance

The Perfect Sub

"The characters are fabulous! Tide and Landon are as perfect as ever for each other. I love how they complement each other in all aspects of their relationship."

—Diverse Reader

The Luckiest Master

"Great storytelling, lots of sizzling sexy-time, and the sweetest couple you can wish for. Enjoy."

—Three Books Over the Rainbow

The Closet Boy

"Their journey is sweet, hot, sexy and filled with love."

—*Divine Magazine*

The Dom's Way

"It's a playful and kinky journey of the hottest kind!"

—Rainbow Book Reviews

By SEAN MICHAEL

Add Love and Mix
Amnesia
Bases Loaded
Cupcakes
Daddy Needs a Date
First Steps
From the Get Go
Golden
Guarding January
Inheritance
Just the Right Notes
Making a Splash
Of Love
Out of the Past
Perfect 10
Sports Pack (Print Only Anthology)
The Swag Man Delivers
Unlikely Hero
Unto Us the Time Has Come
X-Factor

DREAMSPUN BEYOND
#6 – The Supers

DREAMSPUN DESIRES
#39 – The Teddy Bear Club

IRON EAGLE GYM
The New Boy
The Perfect Sub
The Luckiest Master
The Closet Boy
The Dom's Way
The Eager Boy
The Gentle Dom

Published by DREAMSPINNER PRESS
www.dreamspinnerpress.com

THE GENTLE DOM

SEAN MICHAEL

Published by

DREAMSPINNER PRESS

5032 Capital Circle SW, Suite 2, PMB# 279, Tallahassee, FL 32305-7886 USA
www.dreamspinnerpress.com

This is a work of fiction. Names, characters, places, and incidents either are the product of author imagination or are used fictitiously, and any resemblance to actual persons, living or dead, business establishments, events, or locales is entirely coincidental.

The Gentle Dom
© 2018 Sean Michael.

Cover Art
© 2018 L.C. Chase.
http://www.lcchase.com
Cover content is for illustrative purposes only and any person depicted on the cover is a model.

Trade Paperback ISBN: 978-1-64108-115-3
Digital ISBN: 978-1-64080-480-7
Library of Congress Control Number: 2017917544
Trade Paperback published August 2018
v. 1.0

Printed in the United States of America

This paper meets the requirements of
ANSI/NISO Z39.48-1992 (Permanence of Paper).

Chapter One

BARCLAY WHEELED up to the doors of the Iron Eagle gym for his PT appointment and tried not to sigh.

He could do this. He so could. This was him. Doing it.

Blah.

At least they had wheelchair access and the doors into the gym itself from the lobby were good and wide.

A young man with long dark hair and a striking face was mopping the floor. "Oh! Careful. The floor is damp. Stay left and you should be okay."

"Thanks. I have an appointment with a Reece?"

"I'll tell the front desk." The man went over to the desk. There were two guys, one quite young, behind it, and a tall, stacked guy standing in front of it. That was who looked over, then smiled and waved and came toward him.

You can do this. You got this. This is how you heal.

As the man approached, Barclay could see that he wasn't quite as musclebound as he'd first thought. They were great muscles, though. Which you wanted in a personal trainer, right?

This guy had curly brown hair and bright smile that lit up his face. He moved well too, limbs loose and easy. Barclay imagined the man would do well at parkour; he walked like he had great body control.

"Hey there. You must be Barclay Drambor."

"I am. Hey. Nice to meet you!" He raised one hand in greeting.

"Reece Gordon. But you can call me Rec. You're several minutes early for your appointment. I like that. Shows that you're serious." Rec stood like he felt easy in his skin.

Barclay used to stand like that. When he was standing, that was. He had always liked to be on the move. Fucking chair made that a little hard right now.

"I wasn't sure exactly where I was going." He hated being late, and if he was headed somewhere new, he'd give himself more time than the GPS claimed he needed.

"You didn't have any trouble finding us, though, right?" Rec continued when Barclay shook his head. "Cool. Let's go into the gym, you can see what the setup is, and then I'll do an interview with you—find out where you are in your recovery, what your goals are, how much time you have to put into it, that kind of thing."

"Fair enough. Lead the way." He wanted to get started so he could have that done. It would be easier to keep going than it was to have wheeled in here in the first place.

"You got it." Rec headed to the double doors across the front lobby, hitting the button to open them automatically. "You should be able to make your way around the first floor without any problems. And there are showers on this floor."

"Good deal." He'd shower at home where he felt safe, but it was good to know it was possible to do it here.

"So as you can see, we have a large variety of equipment. We've got freestanding weights as well as the various machines for muscle targeting, and you'll be able to work out every part of your body, even from the chair. There are tons of cardio options as well, including the hand bikes, so you'll be able to get moving there right away too." Rec sat on one of the equipment benches and opened his iPad. "Okay. Let's talk turkey."

"I'm cleared to work out. I broke three vertebrae, but my spinal cord is intact. I broke my left arm in three places, my right leg, and my hip." He rattled his injuries off emotionlessly, like they were someone else's. "I'm ready to get out of the chair."

"Damn, that's impressive. Do you mind if I ask how it happened?" Rec's eyes were hazel—the kind that were almost light brown but for a few flecks of green in them—and they weren't judgy or full of pity.

"I was doing some stunt work and fell off a building. I fell four stories." Fell. Was pushed. Whatever. Rec didn't need to know his theory on that.

"Oh man. I take it you're lucky to be alive, eh?" Rec shook his head.

Yeah, except just alive wasn't anywhere near enough. "That's the rumor. I intend to be back to work." Maybe not soon, but someday.

"Good for you. I'm glad you chose me to help you get there. So what kind of time are you looking at dedicating to this?" Rec pulled up a scheduling app.

"I'm not working right now, and I have some savings. I'm shooting for Monday, Wednesday, Friday." He could do cardio in between just wheeling himself around the block a few times. The chair was surprisingly hard work. He could have gotten one of the fancy electric ones, but that would have been significantly more expensive. Besides, the self-propelled variety were a better workout. That's what he told himself anyway.

"Sounds good. For a half hour to begin with?" Rec suggested. "We can work up from there, add in some cardio in between as you grow stronger."

"Let's do an hour. I can handle it." A half hour three times a week was not going to give him the results he wanted.

"How about we start with a half hour for the first week, and we can talk about turning it into an hour the next week?" Rec countered.

"Fair enough." Barclay needed to get back on the horse, start riding.

"It's good that you're eager, and I understand wanting to put in a lot of work, but if you go at it too hard right off the bat, you risk hurting yourself or aching so badly you don't want to come back." Rec's eyes were kind and his voice deep, even.

He still didn't see any pity there, but he straightened his spine and raised his chin all the same. "I'm not a pussy. I can take it."

"There's nothing weak about taking things slowly and giving your body time to heal, time to get used to redoing things." Rec laid a hand on his leg. "Trust me. I'm on your side."

"Thanks. I'm just… I'm ready. I need to get back to normal." He needed this more than anything. It wasn't only a need to be doing better physically—he *needed* to be able to move.

"I hear you. Pushing too hard, too fast can actually set you back, though. Okay? All right. Are you ready to start now? We can run through the machines we're going to use, see what weights you're good to start at, that kind of thing."

"Yeah. I'm ready. Let's do this." He grabbed his weight gloves out of his pocket, telling himself he wasn't worried.

"All right. You're going to do great." Rec stood and led him over to a machine with a bar currently above his head. "Let's start with ten pounds and see how you do." Rec set the pin to ten pounds and brought the bar down for him. "From your shoulder to your waist."

This should be imminently doable. Barclay got himself in and out of the chair before he could use his legs at all, right?

They got up to forty pounds before Rec stopped him and put it back down to twenty-five. "Okay, I know you want to actually start, so ten reps, rest for thirty seconds, then ten more."

Barclay worked doggedly, refusing to let up, forcing himself to work, to get stronger.

They went through a number of machines, focusing on his arms and torso, back and core before they got to the ones where he'd have to move out of the chair.

He set his brake, his arms shaking hard. "Let me get my crutches."

He pulled out the arm crutches and unfolded them.

"Hold on." Rec put a hand on his arm and shook his head. "I think you've done enough for today. Next time we'll start with your legs so your arms aren't tired."

"You sure? I can do it." He totally fucking could, dammit.

"I'm sure you can. But I'm also sure it'll be a better experience for you if we wait to do your legs next time. You did great here today. I know you think it wasn't much, but it was a lot. And we're already at the half-hour mark."

"Okay." Okay, he guessed it was time to catch a bus and go home. "I'll be back Wednesday, ready to work."

"You need any help with the showers?" Rec asked as they headed toward the locker room.

"I'll just…. It's gonna be slick. I'll take care of it at home." He didn't want to fall again.

"I'm happy to help—no judgment or shame. And there's a wheelchair-accessible stall. If you want—it's entirely up to you." Rec held the door open for him.

"Thanks." He wheeled himself through. "I can probably manage, thanks."

"Probably?" One of Rec's eyebrows went up.

That made him laugh and feel a bit better. "I can totally manage on my own." Especially as he wasn't actually showering.

"Okay, cool. I'll see you on Wednesday." Rec squeezed his shoulder and headed out, leaving him alone in the locker room.

He sat there until someone else came in, then wheeled himself out and headed for the bus stop. His muscles *were* tired, but pushing through all the shit had gotten him this far and he'd be damned if he stopped now.

REC GOT up early on Wednesday morning and went in to put in an hour of weights before his first client. Today was his busy day. He had Allen at nine for an hour and a half. Allen was training for a marathon, and they were building up his endurance. Then he had the new guy—Barclay—at eleven. He was legs today. Figuring out what he could do. Rec suspected today would be harder than their first session because the guy wasn't going to be able to work his lower body muscles as hard as he'd worked his torso and upper body the other day. After that Rec had to head out to the Goodlife Fitness down the road and run three different group classes, and then he had a last client session at eight tonight. Thank goodness they weren't all Wednesdays.

He took a quick shower up on the Doms' floor after his workout and ran into Tyrone in the locker room as he was getting dressed. They exchanged pleasantries and Tyrone seemed to have a few moments, so he decided it was as good a time as any to bring up a proposal he'd been thinking of.

"I wanted to talk to you about maybe putting together some classes." He'd signed on to do the Goodlife ones because he had the time and they were decent money, but he thought that some courses would make a great addition to Iron Eagle's repertoire.

"Classes, eh?" Tyrone leaned against a set of lockers. "What sort of classes?"

"Well, we could do all sorts, depending on what the clientele is looking for. Cardio dance, cardio step, muscle building, stretching. I bet with the obstacle training course out back, you could do a ninja warrior course or two. I think folks would eat that up. You could run a survey to figure out interest."

"That's an interesting idea. I'll suggest it. In the end, it'll come down to what the boss wants, but I'll definitely bring it up. I take it you're interested in teaching if we do put some together?"

Rec nodded. "Oh yeah. I'd love to."

"And you've got some experience with what the routines might look like with these kinds of courses."

"Yeah, I've been doing a few down the road for about six months now." And anything he didn't know, he could totally do research on. Like the ninja warrior course.

"Okay. If you get tagged for actually putting together the courses and setting up the schedules and stuff, it's your own fault." Tyrone gave him a wink.

That had him chuckling. "Gotcha. I hate to propose and run, but I've got to go—I've got a client."

Tyrone waved him off and started stripping out of his street clothes.

Rec pushed Allen hard for an hour and a half, pleased with the progress the guy was making, then did some paperwork as he waited for Barclay to show. He was looking forward to this session, to seeing where Barclay was at with his legs. He knew this was where the real work would be.

The man was a little early again, and that pleased Rec. He liked punctuality and dedication. He liked not having his time wasted, and being on time or early meant he was being respected.

Going over to Barclay, he shook his hand and led the way into the gym. "So how are you feeling? Were you very sore after Monday's session? Any residual soreness?"

"I'm good."

Rec had a feeling that would have been Barclay's answer no matter what the truth was. He'd have to watch and make sure the guy didn't push himself too far. It really would be more of a hindrance than a help. The trick was figuring out where the line lay between working hard and pushing too far.

"You have a good day yesterday?" he asked.

Barclay shrugged. "It was a day. I just want to get back to my old self again."

"You'll get there, I swear. I know these first few weeks are going to feel like you're moving slower than a snail's pace, but they're the foundation for everything else." Dedication and desire would take Barclay far.

"Sure. Yeah." Barclay wore sweats and a T-shirt, the bottoms loose, covering up Barclay's musculature.

Rec already knew that the guy's upper-body muscles were actually pretty good, if a little rusty. They could fix that easily. He suspected Barclay might be doing a bit of free-weight work on his arms at home, and God knew wheeling the chair around could build up more than a little muscle. But Rec had no idea how much work Barclay's legs were going to take until they put in some time.

Rec stopped at the first machine. "Okay. We'll start with your hamstrings."

Barclay grunted and grabbed his crutches. Rec stepped back, knowing his help would not be appreciated. Barclay was clearly determined—and stubborn—and he got himself to the machine. Rec started with five pounds and worked slowly up before cutting the weight back and getting Barclay to do his first rep.

He explained which muscle group each machine worked as they moved through them, though he suspected that Barclay didn't need the lessons. Still, it filled the silence, and Barclay didn't tell him to stop.

Barclay's left leg was much stronger than his right, which, given his injuries, made total sense. Rec made a few notes so he could tailor Barclay's future workouts. He'd put together a set routine for Friday, and once Barclay had run that, he'd know where to tweak it.

By the time the half hour was up, Barclay was clearly done. He nearly fell moving back from the last piece of equipment to his chair. Rec wasn't surprised, and he didn't make a big deal out of it.

He did call a stop to the workout. "Okay, that's our half hour. You did a great job today. It's the first time you've worked those muscles in a long time, and your right side has to relearn everything. I'm really pleased with how much you pushed today."

Barclay snorted, looking less than impressed.

"It's the first time you've worked out your right side since the injury," Rec repeated. "Trust me, you're doing great. I can see that the muscle you're going to be working out the most is your patience."

Barclay actually laughed at the joke, looking almost surprised at himself. Rec clapped him on the back.

"Did you need help getting to the locker room or dealing with the shower?" He liked to be early for his classes at the Goodlife, but he certainly had time to give a helping hand if it was needed.

Barclay refused, just as he'd done on Monday. Rec did make sure he made it to the locker room okay. He didn't offer to push the chair there—he was pretty sure his offer would be refused and Barclay would be affronted.

"I'll see you on Friday, then."

"I'll be here," Barclay assured him.

"Good. I've got to get going so I'll leave you to it." He gave Barclay's shoulder a squeeze. There was something about Barclay that drew him in, made him want to get to know the guy better, to get more than a few words out of him.

He's a client, Rec reminded himself as he headed out. Still, he couldn't shake the feeling that Barclay needed him as more than just a personal trainer.

BARCLAY ARRIVED at the gym, raring to go despite his right leg still feeling a little sore from Wednesday's workout. Rec had obviously put together a routine based on what they did Monday and Wednesday, because he knew exactly what machines and how many reps of each he wanted Barclay to do.

Barclay worked for nearly an hour too, not backing down when Rec kept moving from machine to machine, even when he started to feel shaky. If the last few machines hadn't been accessible from his wheelchair, he wasn't sure he would have been able to make the trip from his wheelchair to the apparatus.

He would never have said anything, but he had to admit to being happy when Rec called a halt to the day. He wheeled himself into the locker room and just sat for a second, head down as he breathed.

"Barclay? Hey. It's all right. It's going to be all right. You're going to get there. It's going to take work, but you are."

"I'm okay. I'm cool. Super. I just. I'm cool."

"When was the last time you had a meal out?" Rec asked, the question coming out of left field.

"Pardon me?" Had he heard right?

"Let's go have lunch. Talk. Do something normal, you know?"

"Why?" He blinked at himself. *Jesus, Barclay. Don't be a fucker. You love making friends, meeting people.* At least he had up until fifteen fucking months ago. "God, that was rude. I'm sorry. If we can go somewhere super casual, I'd be happy to. I swear I'm not bad company, as a rule."

Rec laughed and slapped him on the shoulder. "No problem. It's maybe been a while since you did something normal like go to a restaurant, eh? There's a Swiss Chalet just around the corner. You like chicken?"

"Chicken is fine with me." Although he could murder a smoothie. He loved the quick energy spike he got from them. They felt good going down too.

"Cool. You want to take a shower first or you want to just go? I'm easy either way."

"Let's just go. I'm passable, and this is a gym, right?" He wasn't going to mention that he had yet to use the gym's showers.

"You're totally passable. Let's go. I'm starving."

"Yeah." Barclay wheeled himself out, focusing on steady and sure, on control. He ignored how tired his muscles were. A meal and a bit of time would have him right as rain before he had to get himself home.

They went right out of the gym, and sure enough, the Swiss Chalet was half a block down. It took them all of a minute to get to it. Rec held the door open for him.

"Thanks."

They found a table, and he stayed in his chair instead of trying to switch. No way was he going to risk looking like a fool.

They'd barely even opened their menus when their waitress showed up. "Hey, guys. Can I get you something to drink?"

"I'll just have water, please," Rec answered.

"Uh." He wanted juice or a smoothie, but that wasn't here. "Do you have lemonade?"

"Sure thing, hon. I'll give you guys a few minutes with the menu, and I'll bring your rolls with the drinks."

"Thank you." Rec met his gaze when she left. "We should probably look so we're ready when she comes back."

"Right." Barclay stared at the menu.

"I know I should order the breast, but I really like the leg." Rec looked torn. "Although, as I'm going to be eating all the skin—because yes, yum!—I suppose it doesn't matter whether I have the dark or the light meat after that."

"I'm going for the pasta."

"I've never had the pasta here," Rec admitted as he put aside his menu. "So are you a pasta fan because you like it or because you need the carbs?"

"Because I need the carbs. I mean, I like pasta better than rice, and I'm hungry."

"That's cool." Rec pointed at the chair. "So how long ago did it happen?"

"Fourteen months, two weeks, three days, fifteen hours."

"Over a year? No wonder you're chomping at the bit to get into the gym."

"Yeah. I was in the hospital a while." And then at his folks'. Finally he was on his own. It wasn't pretty, but it had felt good to get out of his folks' place. He loved them, but he was an adult; they weren't supposed to be taking care of him anymore.

"You've come for my guidance now, though. And you made it past the first and second session and actually showed up for the third. That's how you know you're really on the mend." Rec gave him a wink.

He didn't know that he had a choice. He wasn't ready to do something else—he needed to get back to work. "A friend of mine recommended you. He says you're the best in the business."

"Oh now, you've got to let me know who I have to thank." Rec had a great smile.

"Tide Germaine. I know him professionally, and we happened to meet at the coffee shop a few weeks ago." It had been well-timed as he'd been going in for his all clear to begin working out the following week. So he'd asked.

Rec's smile turned into a beam. "I'll definitely have to thank him for that. He's a great guy."

"He is. Hell of a hard worker." Hot too, but not really Barclay's type—a few too many muscles. He liked them a little leaner, more like Rec.

"He does the gym proud, that's for sure."

Their waitress came with their drinks and the promised rolls and butter. "You guys ready to order?"

They ordered their meals, and when the waitress left again, Rec grabbed a roll. "Oh man, these are still warm. I love that."

Barclay took one, ate it because his body was demanding fuel. When he broke it open, steam escaped and the butter melted beautifully on it.

"Good, eh?" Rec asked, offering him a smile, this one full-on directed at him.

"Yeah. I'm starving, man." He grabbed his lemonade and downed three-quarters of it.

"I'm not surprised, given the exercise. You might find yourself hungrier now that you're working out regularly. It's a signal to your body that you're serious about being well. Plus, you know, actually burning calories."

"Yeah." He'd been doing body-weight stuff for a few months with a couple free weights, but at his own pace and just his arms.

"So you're a stuntman?" Rec asked.

"Yeah. I mean, I'm not working right now, obviously, but I'll be back to it soon." He didn't know anything else. The other option was living in fear that Duncan was going to come back and finish the job, and Barclay wasn't going to do that.

"You will be. I've seen how motivated you are, how willing to put in the work. So what was supposed to happen when you jumped? Did you miss the bag or something?"

"There wasn't a bag. I wasn't supposed to fall."

"Oh. Oh man." Rec winced. "So why did you?"

Barclay shook his head. "I don't remember."

It was a lie, at least partially. He didn't remember much, and he wasn't sure if what he did remember was correct. But he didn't fall. That hadn't been what happened at all; he was pretty sure of that.

"That sucks. Hell, the whole thing does, doesn't it? But it's getting better. You'll be jumping off roofs on purpose in no time, I bet."

"Yeah. I bet." Even if the thought made him sick to his stomach right now. "I can't wait."

"So what have you been doing with your time? Pick up any interesting hobbies?" Rec buttered himself another roll.

"I surf a lot, I guess. Sleep a lot." His days and nights were all messed up, totally backward. Having to come into the gym three times a week at a set time was actually his first taste of having a routine again, and he liked it. It felt like a step in the right direction anyway.

"You miss being active, eh?"

"Sure. I used to be going going going. I'm"—*bored*—"getting back to it."

Rec chuckled. "You're bored. I get it. It would drive me nuts to not be able to do my job."

It sounded like Rec understood, given he'd known Barclay was bored without him having to say it. That was good, right? If Rec understood how this had set his entire life on its head, every bit of it.

"Yeah. Well, my goal is to be out of the chair next month and back to work in three months."

"That might be pushing things a little, but I will do my best to get you there. Safely," Rec added.

Barclay wasn't interested in safe; he just didn't want to keep on dying.

"So what kind of movies do you like?" Rec asked, looking like he was actually interested rather than just making conversation.

"Action-adventure. I watch some horror. I'm pretty easy, assuming there's something going on to watch."

"While it's not the only thing I watch, I'm a huge fan of all the comic book adaptations. I do marathons on a regular basis." Rec talked with his hands a little when he became animated.

"Yeah? That's cool. Which one's your favorite?"

"I've got to go with the Thor movies. He's yummy. Plus, I like the stories. And the brother. Mmm Loki." Rec winked at him.

Wait. Was Rec flirting with him?

"Yeah. Yeah, he's got that skinny evil thing going on." The guy playing him could act his way around everyone else too, which didn't hurt.

"He does indeed."

Their waitress returned again, this time with their food. "You guys need anything else?"

Rec glanced at him, then shook his head. "I don't think so—this looks pretty good as is."

"Wave me down if you change your mind." She headed over to another table, the place getting busier with the lunch crowd coming in.

"It does look good." Barclay dug in, finding that the pasta needed a load of salt and pepper. That was par for the course when it came to restaurant pasta. He ate quickly, his belly demanding he feed it.

Rec pulled the skin off his chicken and set it to the side before devouring his meat, then his fries, then his coleslaw, in that order. When he was done with everything else, Rec ate his skin, moaning over it. "God, I love this stuff." It was the first thing he'd said since they started eating. They'd both been focused on stuffing their faces.

"It's probably bad for you," Barclay teased.

"Are you kidding? It's the worst. That's why it tastes so damn good." Rec laughed, eyes dancing. "Pretty much everything good is bad for you."

"No shit. I'm ready to be back to work so I can eat whatever I want."

"You a fan of popcorn?" Rec asked as he finished his water off.

"I guess, yeah. The more butter the better."

"That's how I like it too. You should come over this weekend and we'll do a Marvel movie marathon." Rec definitely had to be flirting with him.

"Are you flirting with me? I mean, are you?" He didn't want to get it wrong.

Rec smiled, but it wasn't mocking, it was warm, kind. "I am. Is that terribly unprofessional of me? I don't think so. I mean, I'm only your trainer a few hours a week. And you're hot."

"Okay, that's good to hear. Thank you. I'm not sure I'm ready to talk about dates, but flirting, that I can handle." He thought.

"Then you'll come to the movie marathon?" Rec asked, quickly adding, "It's totally not a date. Just two guys hanging out together, watching hot guys beat things up."

"We'll share numbers and, if you don't get a better offer, sure." Or Barclay decided not to leave his house ever again. There was a good chance it could happen. It did a fair bit.

"I'm not going to get a better offer. If you're worried about getting around, I could bring the movies and popcorn to you."

"No. No, I have…. It's cool." His place was a wreck and sad, and he didn't let anyone come in.

"Excellent. Then it's a date. Or not a date—a get-together. I'll give you my address, and you can come around ten or eleven?" Rec was a pushy bastard.

"If you're sure. What… what should I bring?"

"Drinks? I'm partial to green tea lemonade."

"Green tea lemonade. Okay." He'd pick some up at the store on the way.

"Awesome. And whatever you want, of course. We'll order a pizza when we get sick of popcorn." Rec looked pleased.

"I'll have to look at the bus schedules, see how long I can stay."

"Oh, a marathon means late into the night. The couch pulls out into a bed. You can totally stay." Rec wasn't giving up or letting him use easy excuses, it seemed.

"That's a little far, isn't it? For a nondate."

"A date would not involve pulling out the couch," Rec noted drily.

Barclay's cheeks heated, and he suddenly couldn't meet Rec's eyes. Christ. Just tell the man yes and then cancel.

"Look, I think you could use the day out of your apartment, out of your head, and watching movies is always better with someone else. Say yes already." Definitely a pushy bastard.

"Sure. Just let me get your number, huh?" There. That wasn't a definite yes, but it should placate Rec.

"No problem. Give me your phone and I'll put it in your contacts. Meantime, you want some dessert?"

He looked out the window toward the sky, which was clouding up but not ready to rain, not yet. "Maybe, yeah. Yeah." He was definitely hungrier than he'd been before he'd finally started working out for real again.

"Yeah, me too. I love the pecan pie. And the coconut cream pie. And the new cinnamon doughnuts are pretty good. I come here just for dessert sometimes, especially if I only have a little time between clients. I wind up spending a lot of time in the gym to make up for it."

"I've never met a doughnut I didn't like," Barclay admitted.

"I'm more a cakes and pie man, but I hear you. Besides those little cinnamon doughnuts are pretty much cake." Rec laughed. "One of the guys at the gym—well, Tide actually—he makes fun of my sweet tooth."

"He seems pretty strict, yeah." The man was stacked to high heaven, and you could tell just by looking at him there wasn't a bit of fat on the amazing body. Barclay had seen him eating a few times too—not a single carb had passed Tide's lips on any of those occasions.

"Oh, he's a good guy. He likes everyone to think he's all tough, but really, if you see him with his bo—his Lance, you can see he's a softie."

"Is Lance the photographer? He was sweet to me." Hadn't pitied him either, which was always a plus in Barclay's books.

"Lance is the photographer. I'm glad he was good to you. I take it you met him when you first inquired about a personal trainer?" Rec raised his hand to get their waitress's attention, nodding when she indicated she'd seen them.

"Just briefly. He was heading out for a shoot as I was rolling in."

"He's a good guy—works out on the ninja warrior course behind the gym. In fact, I think it was built with him in mind. Not that it isn't getting a lot of use, but Tide may have pushed for it just for Lance." Rec put his number in Barclay's phone and handed it back to him.

"I wanted to be on that show, once upon a time. Maybe next year." He'd always been working when the tryouts had rolled around, though, so he'd never investigated going as a Canadian.

"I thought maybe that was your kind of thing. I also think maybe graduating to that equipment would be a good incentive—something to work toward." Rec pointed at Barclay's phone. "If you send me a text, I'll have your number too."

"Right." He sent a text with his name and a smiley face.

Rec checked his phone and laughed softly. "That's great."

Their waitress finally came back to clear their plates. "Can I get you some dessert or coffee?"

"Yeah, we'd like some dessert, please. A piece of pecan pie and the doughnuts." Rec glanced at him. "You want to try anything else? If we share, it's not even like we're having a complete dessert on our own."

Except that they were having two of them.

"No, that's plenty. Seriously."

"Good choice! You passed the test." Rec gave him a wink before telling their waitress that the two desserts were all they needed.

"There was a test?" Hell, he knew how much work he needed to do to make up his calories.

Rec chuckled and shook his head. "Nah. Not on your first week. And I'd totally buy you an extra dessert if you wanted one."

"I'm really okay." He found a smile. God, he was suddenly pooped. Worn out. Like the food had reminded his body that he'd just worked out and needed to nap now he'd refueled. He was glad they were doing dessert so he didn't have to get himself home yet.

"Cool." Rec tilted his head. "If it's not too forward to ask—how are you getting home?"

"The bus. I live about two kilometers from here. I can wheel it, but it's a challenge." A challenge he wasn't up to after working out.

"And not right after working out," Rec noted, echoing his own thoughts. "Especially your first day doing the full routine. I could push you, though. No offense intended, but I thought food would perk you up a bit, but you honestly don't look up to the bus."

"Do I look that bad? Really?"

"You don't look bad—you look tired. I'm comparing from when you first came in earlier. You seem a little pale now." Rec shrugged. "It wouldn't be any bother—I'm planning a run this afternoon anyway, so a brisk walk as warm-up would be cool."

"I wouldn't mind the company, I guess." Or the help. If he wasn't putting Rec out, which it seemed he wasn't.

"Great! I'd just hate to abandon you to the bus when it's not necessary."

Rec turned his attention to the waitress as she came back with their desserts. "You can put them in the middle—we're going to share."

"Sure. You guys enjoy." The waitress nodded at them, smiled, then walked away.

"We will enjoy, hmm?" Rec offered Barclay a fork, then stole one of the doughnuts, dipping it in the caramel sauce and popping the whole thing into his mouth.

"How's the sauce?" Barclay took one doughnut and split it with his fork. It was crispy on the outside and cakey on the inside, and best of all, it was still piping hot, steam rising from where he'd split it.

Rec swallowed before saying "Delicious."

Barclay tried a little bit, finding that the salt cut the sweet just enough. He went back for a bigger bite the second time and dunked it in the caramel sauce.

Rec smiled as he ate it. "Good, eh? For a doughnut. You'll have to try the pecan pie next."

"It's good, yeah. I like it. Of course, doughnuts are good." He had yet to meet one he didn't like.

Rec took one of the forks, cut off a piece of pie and stabbed it. Then he handed the fork over to Barclay. "Tell me this isn't even better."

"Thank you." He tried it, the caramelized sweet just lovely. Not as good as the doughnuts, but very tasty nonetheless.

Rec grinned. "You like it—I can tell."

"What's not to like, right?"

"Exactly!" Rec laughed, looking pleased, happy. It made him easy to be around.

They ate the desserts—Barclay had a bit more than half of the doughnuts, and Rec had the lion's share of the pie, but eventually they'd destroyed both and were licking their fingers and wiping their mouths with their napkins.

Their waitress brought over the bill without being prompted—no doubt trying to stay ahead of the rush, and Rec pulled out his wallet. "We'll need the machine, please."

She pulled it out of one of the deep pockets of her apron and grabbed the bill back, entering in the total.

"I have some cash. I can get my half," Barclay offered. He wasn't a charity case.

"If you want. I'm easy." Rec handed his card over. "Twenty bucks'll cover your half plus tip."

Barclay handed the twenty to Rec, then leaned over to put his gloves back on. He might take company on his "walk" home, but he wasn't getting pushed, even if Rec had offered earlier. Now that the time had come, he could do this.

Rec dealt with paying, then got up, and they headed for the street again. "You want me to push your chair?"

"I got it. We're good." He had his pride, after all, and the food and rest had helped with his muscle fatigue. The fact that he'd consumed a large amount of sugar probably wasn't hurting any either.

"Sure, no problem. Lead on."

He put his head down and headed up the street, which had a subtle hill that you really noticed when you had to propel yourself up it in a wheelchair. He moved doggedly, counting out a steady rhythm.

"You never mentioned you had to go up the hill," Rec noted. "There wouldn't be any shame in me giving you a bit of a push."

"I think everywhere in this town is up a hill somehow." He'd never really noticed before his accident. And to make it worse, none of it was steep, which made him feel like a wimp.

Rec chuckled and dropped behind him. "Let me help you out until we're past the uphill, okay?"

He would have argued, but he was going to hurl if he continued to propel himself, no question. No question.

When he didn't say anything, Rec murmured, "Watch your hands," and started pushing him. Thank God.

He closed his eyes for a second, letting himself just breathe through the exhaustion and hoping the need to barf backed off.

"Just let me know where to go," Rec said.

"I'm in the big blue complex on the left at the very top of the hill." Just where it started getting easier again.

"Cool. What floor are you on?"

"The first. I'm all the way in the back, but I'm on the first floor, thank God." Even now he wouldn't survive a climb of any sort, let alone when he'd actually rented it.

"No elevators, eh? I know a lot of these older places don't have them." Rec turned into the walkway of his apartment.

"No." He was living careful. Real fucking careful. What savings he had needed to last until he was well enough to be earning again. Which was why he had a one-bedroom in an older place where his chair barely fit down the halls.

"They've got charm, though." Rec waited for him to unlock the door, then wheeled him in.

"Ignore the mess, please." He was trying his best, but… well, depression was a bitch, and that went double on the disabled list.

Rec snorted. "I'm a guy who lives alone. I know from messy."

"It's just…." It was rough.

"Hey." Rec crouched next to him and put a hand on his knee, warm and solid and comforting. "Whatever it is, it's okay. You can tell me."

"I'm fine. I'm really fine. I just… I have a learning curve." He couldn't reach anything. He fell a lot. He was scared to stand in the shower. What if he fell and reinjured himself and couldn't get up? Who knew how long he'd be stuck on the ground?

"Of course you do. And I bet that curve just keeps returning whenever you reach a new plateau. I'm here to help, Barclay. I'm not going to judge," Rec assured him.

"You don't have to. I do." And he knew how far he had to go to get back to where he'd been. *He* did. Not Rec. Not anyone else.

"I think maybe you're judging yourself harshly, aren't you?" Rec asked.

"I don't know." He hadn't been expecting someone to talk to him, to pay attention. That was new.

"That's fair. Come on, show me around your place. I won't promise not to notice any mess, but I will promise not to care."

"I…. There's not much to see." He had the couch, a TV, a mattress on the floor, and that was it. He didn't bother with a table or a dresser or anything. They would have just gotten in the way. He could barely reach the counter with the stove and kept his dry goods and dishes in the two lower cupboards. He didn't really need more than the bare bones anyway. His prized possession was his laptop, which provided most of his entertainment.

Rec frowned. "Was this your place before you got hurt?"

"No. No, of course not. I lived in a loft downtown." It had still had a hefty mortgage on it, though, so he'd sold it, as it had not been wheelchair friendly.

"I can see how that would make it hard to get around. Why didn't you keep it? Your mattress could have gone on the floor there, couldn't it?"

"I couldn't afford it. I went from good money to no money, huh?"

"That sucks hard." Rec squeezed his leg. "I suppose you'd like me to get out of your space already, eh? You're still coming to mine for that movie marathon tomorrow, right?"

"Sure. Sure. Just text me the address, huh?" He was totally cancelling. He would just hide until Monday when he had to go back for his next session.

"I will. Anytime after eleven. Thanks for hanging out with me for a while, B."

"Thank you for everything. You've been incredibly kind." And he hadn't experienced a lot of kindness since leaving his folks' place and moving back out on his own.

"Hey, my pleasure. I will text you my address—I hope you'll come."

Barclay reached out, shook Rec's hand. It was warm, and he let it go with a strange reluctance. He'd forgotten how good it was to have human contact, connection. "Have a good run, man."

"Oh, I will. Downhill all the way." Rec gave him a wink and a wave and was gone.

Barclay closed the door, shaking his head. God, he was tired. He rolled himself over to the mattress and locked the wheels on his chair. He managed to get out of the chair and dropped down onto the mattress, where he let himself collapse with a groan. He didn't even bother to shift himself into the middle of the thing. It wasn't going anywhere, and he could do it later.

He closed his eyes and worked on emptying his mind. He'd go back out Monday. Until then, he wasn't dealing with anything.

Chapter Two

REC WOKE up Saturday morning and went for another run—just five kilometers this time—then did a quick cleanup of his little condo. He was on the eighth floor, but was on the side with the view of the street, not Lake Ontario. It was amazing how much more expensive the lakeview apartments were. There was only his bedroom, bathroom, kitchen, and living room, so it didn't take long to clean.

He put some drinks in the fridge in case Barclay forgot, double-checked not only his popcorn supply, but also his popcorn topping supply. He was good. He even had a bit of cinema-style candy to put out in his cereal bowls. Mike and Ikes went great with popcorn. Then he pulled out all his Marvel movies, queuing up *Iron Man*, as that was the first one. Not his favorite, but if you were going to do a marathon, that meant you watched them all, and in order.

At ten thirty, as he lounged on his couch flipping through TV channels while he waited for Barclay, the text came.

Hey man, I don't think I'll make it. I'm sore & having trouble. Sorry.

Damn. He wondered if Barclay really was that sore, or if it was just hard for him to get out to spend some time with someone he didn't know that well. Rec knew that wasn't always an easy thing to do, especially coming off pretty severe injuries. Barclay had to be seeing himself as *not* himself.

He texted back, *come get you?* Then all Barclay would have to do was sit. On the comfy couch even.

don't want to put you out

sitting here with nothing to do but watch movies—not putting me out

Come on, come on, Barclay, Rec thought. *We could be great friends. Maybe more. Give me a chance.* He waited for the response.

u dont mind?

Score.

nope on my way

Rec tossed on some clean running gear, put his earbuds in, and headed out. He was in the opposite direction from the gym, but it only added a kilometer or so to the distance.

It was a good run, easy and steady, and by the time he got to Barclay's apartment, he was feeling good, loose. He knocked on Barclay's door, jogging in place so he didn't cool off. He had a hunch Barclay might enjoy it if he ran while pushing the wheelchair—give the man a chance to go fast.

Barclay opened the door looking utterly exhausted, huge dark circles under his eyes. Rec schooled his expression not to show his dismay and wished he'd insisted on pushing from earlier on yesterday. At least Barclay could sleep through the movies and not have to worry about making himself food. Not eating would not help Barclay out any, but Rec suspected when the guy was this tired, making food, even something simple, would seem like an enormous task.

"Hey—you ready for a ride over to my place?" He kept moving.

"Hey. Are you sure? I'm just… I'm more sore than I'd expected. One day I'll get a place with a hot tub."

"They're putting in some hot tubs at the gym. I think they said they wanted them in by fall, so you'll be able to take advantage of them." He offered Barclay a warm grin. "And yeah, I'm sure. It's not like a movie marathon requires anything but sitting. You can take a couple Tylenol for your soreness and relax all day. It'll be easy fun that won't put any extra strain on your muscles. Sound good?" He knew he was being pushy, but he honestly thought not being alone would be good for Barclay, and it wasn't like the guy was going to have to do anything once he was there, or even to get there for that matter.

"Are you…? You're being really nice to me. Thank you."

He appreciated Barclay's catch. He might have growled if Barclay had asked yet again if he was sure. And Jesus, had no one ever done anything neighborly or friendly for Barclay in far too long or what? "You're welcome. There aren't a ton of people I connect with, and I liked you on sight. Friends are good to have."

"They are. I don't have many left."

"Yeah, something like this happens and you find out who your real friends are, eh?" Rec put a hand on Barclay's shoulder and squeezed.

Injuries like Barclay's were isolating because he couldn't go out and do the things he used to, even simple things like hanging out at the coffee shop with friends.

Rec waited for Barclay to lock his door before grabbing the back of the chair and wheeling him down the hall.

"You don't have to…."

Right, like Barclay could manage wheeling himself around at this point. Besides, this was supposed to be a no-energy-needed day.

"But I want to. I thought you'd enjoy the ride if I go ahead and run back home. Is that good with you?" It would surprise the heck out of him if Barclay said no.

"Okay. Okay, sure. It might be fun."

"You shout out if suddenly it's not." He didn't expect there would be any requests for him to slow down or stop, though. He thought maybe someone needed to fly a little bit.

He pushed them sedately until they were on the sidewalk, made sure it was fairly clear sailing, then said, "Here we go!" before he began to really move, starting off at a medium jog to let Barclay get used to the speed. Barclay didn't seem the least bit worried. In fact, he leaned forward, into the wind.

Excellent. Rec put on speed, slowly getting up to a comfortable run. They weren't going so fast people couldn't get out of their way, and the lights were with them so they didn't even have to stop at the roads. Thank goodness for sidewalks that had ramps to get to the road.

By the time they got to the gym, Barclay was laughing, the sound ringing out. Rec approved.

He waved at Tide, Lance, Tyrone, and Bran as they went by, the foursome chatting by the doors to the gym. He laughed too at the surprised looks they got. They had to be quite the sight, him in his running gear, Barclay in his wheelchair, his crutches sticking up from their pocket on the back corner of the chair. Rec kept going, weaving through any pedestrians who didn't jump out of the way. They did a little better when they turned the corner, his street less populated.

It looked like it would be clear sailing all the way to his place. "You ready for some real speed, Barclay?"

"Yes! Yes, please!"

He brought Barclay out onto the bike lane on the road so they could avoid up and downs and pushed his speed so they were flying along.

Barclay let go of the arms of the chair and raised his hands as if he were on a rollercoaster.

Rec waited until they'd safely crossed the last road, then sped up to his top speed, going hell for leather for the last few hundred meters.

They were both breathless when he stopped them—Barclay from laughing, him from the run. Rec was really pleased by how smoothly that had gone. "Oh God, that worked better than I thought it would."

"That was fun!" Barclay looked over his shoulder with a grin. It lit up Barclay's entire face, making him look both younger and less exhausted.

"You should come with me on my runs more often." That smile was something else. Stunning, really.

"Maybe one day when I'm running on my own, huh? Soon?" There was a wistful note in Barclay's voice. Having to come back from an accident like Barclay's would have been hard for anyone, but having to be as inactive as Barclay had for more than a year when you did a job with such physicality added a psychological aspect to the recovery. It wasn't easy to suddenly no longer be in command of your body.

"Yeah. Real soon. Meanwhile, we have movies to watch." He unlocked the front doors and pushed the wheelchair into his building and over to the elevator. He hit the up button.

"You have an elevator. Cool. Seriously."

"Yeah. We'd have had a shit time if we had to get you up eight flights." In fact, he probably wouldn't have invited Barclay in the first place if that had been the case, and he was pretty sure even if he had it would have been a deal breaker. No way would Barclay have let him carry the man up all those stairs. And not doing this movie day would have been a shame. Not just for Barclay but for himself as well.

Rec wheeled Barclay in after the doors slid open, and pressed eight.

"You would have had to holler down what was on the television."

He laughed, pleased that not doing this at all hadn't been where Barclay's focus had gone. Making jokes was a good sign. "Can you imagine? The neighbors would have had a horse."

"Yeah, maybe you could have used your phone to call it down," Barclay suggested.

This was a charming side of Barclay, and Rec was glad he'd teased it out. Run it out? Either way, he wanted this happy man to stick around.

"Well, we don't have to worry about it. We're elevator ho!" Barclay shouted the last word out.

Rec laughed as the elevator dinged at Barclay's shout. He kept laughing as they worked their way down the hall to his condo. Once he'd unlocked it, he wheeled Barclay in. "Ta-da!"

Barclay looked around, eyes going to the big windows and lingering there a moment. "Nice place, man. I swear, I'll take the bus home tonight and not be a bother."

"Don't worry about it. Like I said, the couch totally is comfortable enough to sleep on if it becomes necessary." He knew the bus schedule was crap on the weekend. And he didn't want Barclay to feel like he had to take off early or anything. Rec was ready for a full weekend movie marathon.

"Thanks." Barclay shook his head a little. "Where do you want me?"

"You want to transfer to the couch? I bet that'll be the most comfortable."

"Sure." Barclay moved over next to it and set his brakes, then pulled out his crutches and took the few steps over to the sofa. Christ, that looked painful. Rec didn't say anything, though, not wanting to bring attention to it. If Barclay wanted to share with Rec, he would.

Once Barclay was settled, Rec put the wheelchair in the corner near the door where it wouldn't be in the way. His halls were pretty wide, so using the chair to get to the bathroom would not be a problem. "You just yell when you need it."

"Sure. Thanks. I'll buy dinner if you want, since I flaked on the drinks."

"That works. Hopefully you like what I've got in the fridge. Speaking of, let me get the popcorn on and get you a drink." His little kitchen was separated from the living room by a bar, which was nice for entertaining. Not that he did a lot of that, but he was pleased about it now as it would let their conversation flow freely.

"Thank you. For everything. Seriously."

"My pleasure. Now drinks." He went to the kitchen and opened the fridge door. "You want a Coke? Juice? Mango ice tea? Lemon ice tea? Or water?"

"Juice?"

Rec thought it was a good choice—plenty of sugar in the juice to help give Barclay a boost. "Sure thing. I've got apple and cranberry."

"Cranberry, please. I love the sour."

"Good choice." He put a bunch of popcorn in the popper, then grabbed a bottle of cranberry juice and brought it out. "You got a preference on toppings? Along with butter, I've got a bunch of Kernels' flavors."

"Whatever your favorite is. I'm easy."

"My favorite changes, but right now it's the white cheddar. I guess it depends on my taste buds' moods." He laughed at himself and found the bottle with the white cheddar powder. "Can you reach the remote from where you are?"

"Yeah. I can wait for you, though." Barclay looked more relaxed already. Without the pinched features, he looked less tired too.

"Sure." Rec put the popcorn in one big bowl and poured melted margarine over it, then added the flavoring. He had a few pieces—quality control and all. Then he headed back to Barclay. "Here we go."

"Smells nice. Thank you." Barclay held himself carefully, leg muscles jumping and leaping restlessly. No wonder the guy looked tired—Rec had a hunch that might be keeping Barclay awake.

He sat next to Barclay and grabbed the remote, turned the TV on. "You okay?"

"I am. Sorry. I can't stop it."

"Your physiotherapy ever include massage?" What those poor muscles needed was some ease.

"No. I learned to deal with it. It's just distracting at first."

That was crazy. "Well, if you want, I could give you a massage in between movies. Or during any slow bits."

"I'm fine. I'll hold them down." Barclay grabbed his quads and squeezed them, the big muscles stilling.

"You see? They need a massage." Rec leaned over and rubbed one leg, letting the warmth of his hand seep in past the sweats. "I don't mind, honest." He couldn't let someone hurt when there was something he could do. Especially if it was something easy like giving a massage.

"I didn't come over for you to have to work. This is… this isn't cool, man. We're just supposed to be dudes watching a movie."

He lifted his hands and put them up. He hadn't expected Barclay to be quite so prickly. "I don't mind, but if you don't want me to, that's cool." Someone needed a keeper, needed to make Barclay accept help.

"I just… I want to be normal again." Barclay gave him an apologetic look. "Just for a minute."

"Okay, sure." He nudged Barclay's shoulder. "I'll get the movie on and shut up already." He did exactly that: turned the TV on, then the Blu-ray player, and started the movie. "*Iron Man* isn't my favorite—I think Tony Stark is an ass, actually. But it's part of the universe, and I'm a bit of a completist, you know?"

"That makes sense. At least he's easy on the eyes."

Rec laughed. "My favorite is Thor." He may have already told Barclay that, now that he thought about it. Oh well, it bore repeating. "That man is yummy."

"He's stacked, for sure. I've always admired guys that could bulk up."

"You could if you wanted to—though it wouldn't help you in your work or doing the ninja stuff." Stacked muscles were not conducive to parkour. That took a super solid core and more compact muscles.

"I'm not apt to it. I'm naturally lean. It's cool." Barclay shrugged easily. "Everyone wants what they're not."

"I'm in the business of helping folks achieve whatever it is they want." He was pretty good at it too, if he did say so himself, but he knew what Barclay meant. The grass always did seem greener on the other side. Until you got there and realized it was pretty much the same grass.

The movie finally started and Rec settled in, taking a handful of popcorn.

Barclay watched, hands on his thighs, laughing softly at the jokes. Rec found himself splitting his attention between Barclay and the movie, thoroughly enjoying having someone there with him. Barclay looked like a California surfer somehow—towheaded with bright blue eyes, a nice broad set of shoulders, and a teeny-tiny waist.

He was sexy in a casual, delicious way. And he needed a keeper from what Rec could see. There was something vulnerable that called to Rec. Did that make him creepy? Surely not. No, that was in his nature to notice and care. It was a part of his makeup. That was why he was a personal trainer. It was also why he was a Dom.

It was why he was sitting there watching *Iron Man*, trying to figure out how to get Barclay to let him massage those poor leg muscles. Was it really that odd for him to do that for Barclay even though they'd gotten together to watch movies? He didn't think so. On the other hand, he belonged to a community where they were more aware of their bodies and their needs and were always ready to lend a helping hand.

Eventually Barclay began to shift, body searching for comfort, for ease, and Rec knew those poor muscles were screaming again. He put his hand back on Barclay's thigh and squeezed lightly, knowing that and the heat of his hand had to be helping. Maybe he could parlay that into a massage if Barclay's pain was stronger than his stubbornness.

"Oh…." Barclay's groan was pure need.

Damn, he should have done this sooner. Rec kept working that thigh with the one hand, digging his fingers in and insisting that Barclay's muscles ease.

"It…. That… that's nice." That was not a request to stop.

"Cool. I'll just keep doing it, then." Maybe Barclay would let him do a proper job of it before the day was done.

"You sure? Because…." Barclay leaned into it, eyes going heavy lidded. Okay, maybe Barclay would actually let him do a proper job of it now. Rec sure hoped so.

"Yeah, I know it feels good. Finally getting some relief, eh? Don't you worry, I don't mind doing it. I like knowing I'm helping." He kept talking softly, almost randomly. He figured keeping a conversation going might help Barclay feel less weird about it.

Another groan tore from Barclay's throat. "Thank you. God. Thank you."

"You want to sit sideways on the couch for a while? If you rest your back against the arm, I can get your other leg too." He patted his lap, totally willing to have Barclay put his legs over it.

Barclay hesitated for a moment. "It's not too weird?"

"Nope." How long had Barclay been living without touch? Since the accident? Longer? "Come on. Let's do this." He reached for Barclay's legs, helping the guy get them across his lap.

The muscles felt strong, solid, the damage bad but not impossible. Rec worked the muscles in the leg he hadn't touched yet. They were hard, trembling beneath his touch. Poor baby. Someone needed contact.

He kept massaging, but every now and then would simply rub his palm along Barclay's leg, wishing Barclay had worn shorts so he had access to skin. "It's okay. I've got you."

"Sorry, huh? This isn't a thing I do. Let some guy touch me."

"Hey, I'm a professional. Granted not a physiotherapist, but personal trainer's in the same general area, right?" He kept massaging, working them a little harder now that he'd warmed the muscles up. He was going to bring Barclay some relief, dammit.

"Yeah. Yeah, I guess. How'd you get into the job?"

"I started out in premed at university and hated it. But I liked working out, and I liked the sports side of medicine. Personal training seemed like a natural fit and meant I didn't have to do the whole school thing."

"Ah. Cool. That's seriously cool."

"I think my folks were disappointed I wasn't continuing with med school. Mom wanted a doctor in the family." Rec shrugged. It wasn't their life, it was his, and he was happy with what he was doing.

"Huh. They'll get over it." Barclay smiled at him, the look commiserating.

"Yep. She only mentions it twice a day when I go visit them—they're in Halifax now. Dad's half-retired. He was a vet, and he's on the list for shelters. Apparently he gets called out a fair bit and never can manage to turn them down, to hear Mom tell it anyway."

"Ah. Mine are both teachers."

"Yeah? What do they think of your job as a stuntman?" He bet any parent would worry if their kid did the kind of work where you could fall and hurt yourself as badly as Barclay had—or worse.

"They hate it, but they love it at the same time. You know how that is, right? They want you to be safe, but it's a neat thing to brag about to their friends and students."

"I get that. So you don't get hassled every time you call. That's good. Are they in town?" Rec couldn't imagine them letting Barclay go through this on his own if they did.

"They live about an hour away. Just the other side of Hamilton. I stayed with them right out of the hospital."

"They don't have any idea how hard things are you for you right now, do they?" His massage was working—Barclay's muscles beginning to loosen, Rec could feel it. It seemed to be loosening Barclay's tongue too—this was the most information he'd gotten yet.

"I'm okay. I'm okay." Barclay was beginning to shiver.

"Are you cold?" He could grab a blanket if that was the case. Rec had a hunch it was more that the sudden ease of his muscles had Barclay's body confused than he was cold.

"No. Not at all."

"Is anything hurting?" If it wasn't, he was totally putting the shaking down to the sudden and unusual ease of Barclay's muscles and just ignoring it.

"No. No, it's just shaking. I can't help it."

"Okay, no worries, I just wanted to make sure." He turned his attention back to the movie. Oh, he'd missed the middle part while focusing on Barclay. He didn't mind that at all.

Barclay melted into the sofa, eyes on Rec's hands. Rec kept massaging, working all the way down to Barclay's feet, then slowly moving back up to Barclay's thighs. Pretty. Those long legs were damn pretty. Even if he couldn't actually see them. They felt that way, though. He'd bet Barclay was a treat to watch doing parkour.

Rec hummed and danced his fingers over Barclay's sweats, wishing again that they were off, that he was sliding his fingers along skin. The urge to actually see washed over him.

"Have you got scars?" he asked quietly. It would make sense of Barclay did.

"Lots."

"I imagine a lot of them are going to fade over time, aren't they?" There were also oils and crap you could use that did a decent job at helping the skin to heal up.

"I think so, yeah. I mean, I had a bunch before, right? I just have new ones now."

"That's kind of sexy, isn't it? Makes you seem dangerous." He laughed at himself. God, he was a dork.

"Dangerous? Shit, man, I'm just a dude who throws himself off buildings."

"That's kind of hot." More than kind of, really. Okay, so he was a big-time super dork.

"I hope it will be again."

He patted Barclay's thighs. "You'll get there. I know being patient is hard, but I swear if you take the time you need, you'll get there."

"I know. I'll figure it out. I can't do anything else." Barclay's shrug seemed fairly casual, like it wasn't bothering him just at the moment.

"And you don't have to do it alone. You've got people in your corner. A new friend…."

"Thanks, man. Seriously."

"You're seriously welcome." He let his hands rest on Barclay's thighs.

"I…. Dude, I might spring wood. It's been a while."

Rec thought about what to say about that—frankly, he had no problem with it. In fact, he rather liked knowing his touch would be enough to make Barclay hard. "Okay. We said we're friends. I'm happy to be friends with benefits." And he was already semihard himself from the touching, though he'd been ignoring that so as not to make Barclay notice and feel awkward.

"You don't think that's weird? You being my trainer?"

"I don't think it's weird. I can still train you. If it's weird to you, though, if you don't want it… well, I guess then it would be up to you what you'd rather do. Train with me or have benefits with me." He hoped Barclay wanted both.

"I don't know what I want. Shit, when did things get so complicated? I remember when two guys could just fuck."

"Hey, I'm good with that. Wanna get each other off?" Now that they were talking about it, he didn't have a semi anymore, he was going for full-on hard.

"Sure. Sure, I mean, I haven't since the accident, so if it doesn't work, it's not you. It's the back."

Now that surprised him. "You haven't been masturbating?" That was a long time to go without getting any erections.

"Things haven't been working. I mean, I was pretty hurt and I'm tired all the time." Barclay's cheeks went bright red. "I mean… shit. Let's just watch our movie."

"You got it. If things come up…." He kept his hands where they were, thumb rubbing along Barclay's leg. He wasn't going to force it by going for Barclay's junk or anything like that, but if Barclay got hard from his simple touches, well then, that was a different story entirely.

"Yeah."

Rec didn't stress the nerves in Barclay's voice. It was okay. Just breathe. In and out. What happened happened.

He kept his eyes half on the movie, half on Barclay, enjoying the feeling of Barclay's legs beneath his hands. He could feel the strength hidden in the muscles, waiting to be coaxed out again.

At some point, Barclay touched his fingers, returning the caresses, so gently, so carefully.

Rec smiled but didn't say anything, figuring Barclay had to decide for himself if he wanted more than to just watch movies. Rec would admit that he'd be disappointed if they didn't at least try, but this was Barclay's decision and he could exercise that patience muscle he'd told Barclay about.

It was sort of lovely, actually: the waiting, the anticipation. It built slowly, filling the room with this sexual tension that eventually made him aware of each breath he took, of the beating of his own heart. All they were doing was sitting there, his hands on Barclay's legs, Barclay's fingers occasionally touching his, and yet it was some of the hottest foreplay he'd ever indulged in.

At some point they both reached for the popcorn at the same time. Their fingers tangled, and they both gasped.

Rec chuckled, sliding his fingers against Barclay's on purpose. Then he offered the bowl to Barclay, letting him have first choice of what was left.

Barclay met his gaze, then held up a piece of popcorn to his lips. Rec opened his mouth and took the piece, his lips closing over Barclay's fingers. They were salty, but there was a distinct flavor beneath the popcorn and white cheddar taste.

"Is it good?" Barclay asked.

"Yeah. Totally. The popcorn is tasty too." God that was cheesy. Rec grinned, though, going with it. He'd already proven himself to be a dork.

"Cool. Your turn to feed me." Oh. Oh, okay. That was adorable.

Rec grabbed a single piece of popcorn and pressed it gently against Barclay's lips. "Open up."

Barclay did, lips parting sweet and slow, tongue coming out to steal the kernel. Rec groaned, heat flaring in the pit of his stomach, and his cock jerked, making itself known. That was hot as hell, and it was even better when the little pink tongue flicked out to taste his skin.

He let his fingers linger and slide along Barclay's soft lips. There was something super intimate about doing that. How many people's lips did you touch like that? Not too many. Even as many lovers as he'd enjoyed, as many subs as he'd trained and played with, this wasn't something he usually did.

When Barclay kept looking at him, seeming mesmerized, Rec leaned slowly in, giving the guy plenty of time to turn away and duck out of the kiss.

Barclay didn't move away or duck; he just opened and leaned in. Their lips met first, the kiss soft and warm and sexy. Then, taking advantage of Barclay's open mouth, Rec swept his tongue in and tasted.

How lovely. He pushed in, tongue-fucking Barclay's lips. He stared into Barclay's eyes as they kissed, letting his need show. He wanted Barclay and wasn't afraid to have them both know it.

Barclay blushed dark, cheeks burning for him. He took a second kiss, then a third, his hands sliding slowly along Barclay's legs. He was covering the same territory as he had during the massage, but he wasn't touching Barclay like it was a massage anymore. Now he was deliberately seeking to arouse.

He was fairly sure Barclay wasn't thinking about massage anymore either—not now. He let his fingers drift upward, running them along Barclay's hips, then moving to barely touch the man's balls through his sweats.

Barclay's soft little gasp felt damn good against his lips. Humming, Rec slid his tongue along Barclay's, stealing another taste, then another.

His own moans were heartfelt, the need rushing through his veins, and when Barclay stroked his inner thigh, his legs began to shake.

"Barclay." He didn't know what he meant by that—he'd just needed to say the name. It felt right with Barclay's taste on his lips.

"Yeah. Yeah, you feel damn good," Barclay murmured.

"So do you." He pushed Barclay's T-shirt up, searching for skin. He found it, dragging along Barclay's abs. His core was still fairly strong and so pretty.

"Mmm. Yeah." It seemed that Barclay had decided to accept this, to go for it, and it was hot as hell.

Rec took another kiss, exploring the muscles that he could tell were going to be an amazing six-pack soon enough. He loved the feeling of the soft skin beneath his fingertips.

Barclay hummed for him, tongue sliding against his, sweet and wet. Groaning, he pushed higher, searching out Barclay's nipples. Were they sensitive? Not? He couldn't wait to find out. There were so many things to find out. That was one of the best things about a new lover—the sense of discovery.

One nipple was scarred, one wasn't, and the comparison was amazing. He wanted to look, but for now he did so by touch, stroking over one, then the other.

They both drew up, but the scarred one was more stiff, more firm. It fascinated his fingers.

"Do they feel different? When I touch them, I mean." He touched them both again, trying to keep both touches exactly the same.

"Yeah. I had the one pierced. It ripped out. Hurt like a bitch."

"When you fell?" He went back to it, touching the scar again now that he knew how it had happened. He winced. That would definitely have been painful.

"Nope. Fight with a boyfriend."

Rec's eyes went wide. "He ripped it out?" What the hell?

"Yeah."

"Shit. Did you get him on domestic abuse?" Because that wasn't right. Not for a second. Normal people didn't do that kind of shit.

"Nah. It was an asshole thing to do. We broke up."

"I should hope so. I wouldn't stay with someone who did that to me." He pinched the scarred nipple gently. "Is it still sensitive?"

"The other is more, but it's not numb or anything." Barclay arched up, pushed into his fingers. Rec loved the unspoken demand for more. Looked like he didn't need to worry about being gentle with the scarred nipple.

"And you like nipple play." That much was clear from Barclay's reactions to his touches. He moved to pinch the other nipple. It would be easy to get distracted by the interesting sensation of scars under his fingers and wind up neglecting the whole nipple.

"Yeah. I do. I don't mind it at all."

There was a difference between didn't mind and enjoyed. He flicked the right nipple, watching Barclay's face to see if he could tell which one was more true. If he was a betting man, his money would be on enjoyed.

Barclay's body shifted, his face softening. That was better than "didn't mind it." Rec tried a little harder touch, figuring someone who'd worn a nipple ring liked the harsher touches as well as the soft ones.

"Mmm. Pull a little. I don't mind."

Barclay needed to lose the casual "I don't mind" when describing his pleasure level.

Rec tugged even harder, then gave the nip a bit of a twist. Barclay gasped and arched for him, looking a little surprised, but not unhappy. Good. He knew how to take care of someone who needed a bit of a firmer touch.

In fact, he sort of excelled at it.

Smiling down at Barclay, he moved back to the scarred nipple to test its sensitivity, to test if Barclay still appreciated a firm touch there as well. He pinched, lightly at first, but slowly tightening his fingers to increase the sharpness of the pinch.

"Fuck...." Barclay shifted, hips searching fruitlessly for friction.

Nice. Better than nice. Rec covered Barclay's erection with his free hand, pressing against the straining flesh. It was so good, and he could only imagine how much hotter it would be without Barclay's sweats in the way. He pressed harder still, then pinched Barclay's nipple again, layering sensation on top of sensation.

"Oh. Oh fuck yeah. Please. Please, man."

"We should tug your sweats down, B." He knew creaming your sweats was not enjoyable. Not that Barclay couldn't borrow something of his, but he had an ulterior motive—he wanted to see and touch Barclay's erection without the interference of material.

Barclay seemed on board with that. "Yeah. Yeah, give a dude a hand?"

"I've got two and they're all yours." He couldn't hold back his grin as he worked Barclay's sweats down. His noises turned into groans as the hard flesh popped into view. "Very nice."

Rec grabbed hold and stroked, holding that lean prick and petting it. Barclay's eyes went wide and he whimpered.

"Oh God. It's been so long." Barclay panted softly, eyes gone vacant, like all his attention was on the touches on his prick.

Rec was so glad he could give this to Barclay. He liked the guy a lot and being able to help like this was wonderful.

Barclay hummed and arched, trying his best to move into the touches. It didn't look very natural, or comfortable.

"You're not in the best position for that," Rec noted. Barclay was at a disadvantage with his ass on the couch and his legs up higher, across Rec's leg.

"Sorry. Sorry, I just can't... damn."

"Easy. Just let me get you off." He held a little tighter and stroked a little harder, still playing with Barclay's nipples with his other hand. No erections for over a year—Barclay deserved this orgasm and more. And he deserved for it to be great. Not that there really was any such thing as a bad orgasm.

Barclay began to cry out over and over, the soft sounds addictive; Rec wanted to hear more of them. He wanted to hear them a lot. He alternated which nipple he stroked, and every now and then pinched, just to give Barclay some different sensations.

He rubbed his thumb across the tip of Barclay's cock, watching the pleasure chase across Barclay's face. Nice.

"Good hands, man." Barclay bared his teeth a little.

"I like touching. I like touching you." He kept doing it. He wanted to get Barclay off. Really, really.

"Gonna... soon, man. Soon."

"That's the idea, B." Very much the idea. He pressed his thumb into Barclay's slit, a bit harder this time to increase the ache.

"B." Barclay repeated the nickname with a smile, then shot, the act looking as easy as pie.

Rec kept stroking, pulling every last drop of pleasure out of Barclay. "You smell good." It meant they were compatible, that smell.

"I—you—thank you."

He let go of Barclay's cock and patted it gently. "You're welcome. It was my pleasure. Well, both our pleasures."

"Uh-huh. Yes. Totally. Yes."

He chuckled. Barclay was cute when still come-addled. The pinched, worried look was completely gone, replaced with ease and contentment.

Rec leaned in and stole another kiss, keeping it light and lazy. Barclay moaned and kissed him back, tongue sliding against his. Groaning, he grabbed hold of Barclay's tongue and sucked on it as it passed through his mouth.

"Mmm." When Barclay cupped Rec's cock, it startled him, the firm touch surprising but just right.

He didn't let it freeze him for long, and he began to move, helping out and pushing into Barclay's touch.

"Yeah. Yeah, man. Let me have skin?" Barclay asked, voice slightly thick.

"Fuck yeah." Rec grabbed at his jogging shorts, trying to get the strings undone. He should have worn some Lycra workout shorts, but he'd deliberately chosen a pair that wouldn't cling and lovingly outline every inch of his cock.

Barclay grinned, eyes wrinkling at the corners. "Cool."

"Not feeling very cool at the moment. Feeling hot. Needy. Want your hand." He finally got the ties on his shorts undone and raised his ass as he shoved the shorts down.

"I'm on it." Barclay wrapped a hand around his cock and squeezed, jacking Rec nice and slow.

Rec groaned and dropped his head back against the couch. Fuck, it felt good. It had been a while since he'd had a helping hand. "Oh yeah. Don't stop."

"I won't. Promise, man."

"Good man." The words came out husky, betraying how much Barclay's touch was affecting him. Half of him wanted to get off hard and fast, the other half wanted for it to take some time so he could linger, enjoy the pleasure for longer.

Barclay offered his lips for another kiss, and Rec took them eagerly. He delved his tongue into Barclay's mouth, picking up the flavor that was pure Barclay.

"You taste great," he murmured against Barclay's lips before diving back in for more kisses. The sensation of Barclay's hand around his cock merged with the kisses, becoming one sensation. God, Barclay's touches felt good.

And Barclay was generous with them, touching him everywhere, letting him feel it all.

"Gonna make me come." He could tell from the sensation in his balls that it wouldn't be much longer before he shot.

Barclay's soft chuff of laughter wasn't in the least bit mocking. "That's totally the idea, dude."

Rec laughed out loud, and as he did, he came, spunk shooting from him and up over Barclay's hand, adding his scent to the smells of sex on the air....

"Mmm. Better, huh?" Barclay's touch eased up, nice and slow.

"Uh-huh. Now I'm feeling melted and lazy. I sure hope you don't want anything, 'cause it's going to have to wait." He was pretty sure his leg bones were currently made of cooked pasta—overcooked pasta at that.

"'M good, man. Just fine. Think the movie's over, though." Barclay pointed at the TV, and now that he was paying attention, Rec heard the repetitious music as the title menu screen played the same twenty-second clip over and over.

"So it is." Grabbing the remote, he turned it off. "I'll get up and put the next one in soon, I swear." He was feeling too lazy to do it right now. He did love that feeling of postorgasmic bonelessness.

"Mmm. I'm good for now. Honest." Barclay looked like how he felt, really.

"Yeah. Me too." Rec chuckled softly. "I'm feeling pretty mellow." He thought he'd needed that, for sure. He thought Barclay had needed it even more.

"Mellow's a good word for it." Barclay cracked an eye open to look at him. "Postorgasmic nap is another."

That had him laughing again. He was discovering that he loved laughing with Barclay. "So you're a come-and-fall-asleeper, are you?"

Barclay pinked—only a touch. "Just been a while, you know?"

"Yeah, you mentioned there hadn't even been any self-love going on since you got hurt. I'm glad to be the one to break your dry spell."

"I appreciate the hand. Really. That was cool." The smile on Barclay's face said it louder than his words.

"It was my pleasure, B. So anytime. Anytime at all." He totally wanted to do it again. And soon. Maybe horizontally next time. With lots more touching. And exploring.

He wanted to play.

Rec could be patient, though. And right now Barclay needed a nap, for more than just the postorgasmic sleepies. Barclay was clearly still honestly tired. No doubt from the twitching and aching in his legs keeping him awake at night.

He switched the tuner to pick up the music from his phone and set it playing something soft and easy. He helped Barclay shift so he was sitting properly on the couch—the armrest really wasn't enough to rest against unless you were actually lying down and not just reclining as Barclay had been. Barclay leaned up against him, the man obviously craving connection. Rec shifted them again, only slightly this time, so they were both more comfortable, and he patted Barclay's side.

They'd watch some more movies after they napped. He dropped his head back against the couch and let his eyes close. He couldn't remember the last time he'd fallen asleep after an orgasm. He was glad this time it was with Barclay.

Chapter Three

BARCLAY WOKE warm and cozy, wrapped around a strong body.

Weird. Nice, but weird. Certainly not a thing he'd done in a long time. He'd forgotten how good it was to wake up and not be alone. Oh, who was he kidding—he hadn't forgotten; he'd pushed it to the back of his mind because he hadn't had any other options.

He shifted, stopping short as he found a kink in his muscles. Ow. He often woke up with aches and pains, but this was a lot sharper—affecting his leg and his back. It was no doubt from falling asleep sitting up and leaning partway over, putting his muscles in positions they hadn't enjoyed in some time.

The body he was wrapped around grunted, a hand petting his hip. "Shh. Shh. Easy now."

"I gotta move. Hurts." Working the muscles was the only way to get the pain to back off—usually stretching to ease the pressure from the unusual position.

Rec popped up immediately. "Damn. Sorry, man. What's hurting?"

"Hip. Hip. Help." He started to flail as each movement intensified the pain and he felt like he was going to fall.

Rec got off the couch and knelt next to him, hands warming his hip right away. Finally, Rec began his massage.

"Oh God. God. Please." Oh, that was better. It usually took ages for him to feel up to moving enough to grab the pain pills he kept by the mattress. Today the pain began to fade at the first touches.

Rec dug in harder, insisting that his muscles ease. "What do you usually do when you have a bad cramp?"

"Yell." A lot.

"That doesn't sound very efficient." Rec gave him a half smile, but he could tease as much as he wanted if he just kept easing Barclay's leg.

"No. But I'm on the floor at least, so that's cool." His pills were usually within reach once he could bring himself to roll over toward them.

Rec snorted. "Doesn't sound cool to me."

"No. It sucks. It hurts." It was what it was, and Rec didn't want to listen to him sitting here and crying like a baby. "Sorry. Whining."

Rec's face was half-twisted, half-frown. "I'll give you a pass under the circumstances."

"The circumstances?"

"Yeah, you know, the falling off the damn roof circumstance."

"Yeah. That one." Barclay didn't want to think about that shit. He especially didn't want to think about how he had "fallen." Or even if he had fallen.

Rec kept working his hip, and Barclay shuddered when it finally gave in to those insistent fingers and eased for him. Rec must have known because he leaned in and kissed Barclay's belly. His lips were soft and warm.

"God. Thank you. Thank you. That was intense. Sorry." He needed to stop being a shit and suck it up. This had been going on for over a year. You'd think he'd be more used to it by now.

"You don't have to apologize for hurting, B. I know you'd rather be doing pretty much anything else."

"Yeah, it's a bitch." And he hated it. He wanted his life back, dammit.

"You're getting better every day, though. And you'll see improvement in leaps and bounds as you strengthen your muscles back up." Rec stopped massaging, leaving his hands on Barclay's hip, keeping it warm. "Better, or do you need more?"

"I'm better. I'm sorry." He needed the bathroom actually. "Can you reach my crutches? I'm going to have to pee." That was the hardest thing at home—being on the floor and having to get himself off the ground and into his chair to go to the bathroom.

"Sure thing." Rec grabbed his crutches in one hand, then offered him the other. "I'll help you get vertical."

"Thanks. Thanks." He grabbed hold of Rec's hand and stood. Then he swayed and found his center before he started the slow, painful trek down the hall. Thank God it wasn't very far. There were plusses to having a smallish apartment, as he knew well himself. Rec's was bigger than his, though. And nicer by far.

Rec saw him all the way to the door. "Just shout out if you need any help," Rec called out as Barclay got the door shut behind him.

He did his business, then eased himself up and back out the door. He needed to go home pretty soon, even if he didn't want to. He didn't want to overstay his welcome, and he wasn't sure exactly what time the buses stopped running on a Saturday night. Hopefully he could get the time schedule online or something before he had to go so he wasn't waiting too long at the stop.

Rec was leaning against the wall a few feet down from the bathroom and had his phone in his hand. "I'm just ordering pizza. I'm getting a meatlovers. What kind do you want? And wings, yay or nay?"

"Gotta love a trainer who provides pizza. That's cool. I love wings." Okay, so maybe he could stay a little longer.

"Hey, I'll help you work it off later." Rec gave him a wink and continued putting the order through on his phone as they made their way back to the living room at his slow-crutching pace. "It should be here within forty-five minutes. You need anything to tide you over?"

"Nah. I'm great, thanks." He sat carefully, then put his crutches out of the way beneath the sofa.

"You want to do *Thor* next?" Rec asked, bending over in front of the TV to take the *Iron Man* disc out of the player.

Oh, that was pretty. "Uhn."

"Is that your comment on the pretty man who plays Thor?" Rec asked, laughing softly.

"Sure." Not a chance. It was all about the man right in front of him. Pretty ass.

Rec bent again, offering him that great view once more, and put the new movie in, then rejoined him on the couch, sitting close. Putting his arm around Barclay's shoulders, Rec tugged him a touch closer. "This good?"

"Yeah. Yeah, it is." It really was. He felt warm, comfortable, solid. Rec was easy to be with and made him feel good. Wanted. He hadn't felt that since longer than he'd been out of commission due to the accident.

"Don't get jealous if Thor gets me hot," Rec teased.

"I can't compete with that big guy, man. No worries." He did stunts because he wasn't talented enough or pretty enough to be an actor. Not that he didn't love his job, because he did. And he wanted to get back to it.

Rec squeezed him gently and pressed their heads together. "Not to mention, you're right here."

What did that even mean? He smiled and leaned harder, letting himself relax.

Rec rested their heads together, seemingly content to watch the movie while they waited for their food. Barclay watched the movie with half an eye, mostly focused on Rec, but also paying attention to how he himself was doing. It was the first time in a long while he'd felt this good in his own skin.

Rec turned to look at him at one point, catching his gaze. Smiling at him, Rec brought their mouths together in slow motion.

Oh. He wasn't sure why he was surprised by the kiss, but he was. It was deep and warm, steady. Rec's eyes were equally warm and steady, looking into him. He felt like Rec really saw him.

He let himself press closer and lean hard, one hand in the center of Rec's chest so he could feel the strong heartbeat. Rec hummed for him, the sound vibrating in his mouth, almost tickling.

Damn, he rarely wanted a twofer, but Rec was inspiring. His cock was already on the rise, like it was trying to get Rec's attention. Stupid body, but damn it felt good to want it. To be hard again. *Again.* How amazing was that after his long drought in that department?

Rec slid his hand across Barclay's leg, moving slowly toward his cock—too damn slowly—and it ratcheted the tension up to the point where he found himself holding his breath as he waited for Rec's hand to finally reach its destination.

Rec chuckled softly, blew into his lips. "Breathe, baby."

He gasped, and air filled his lungs. Oh. Better. He hadn't realized how long he'd been holding his breath.

Rec rubbed their noses together. "It's not going to stop if you take a second to breathe."

"Sorry, man. Just…. Sorry." God, Rec must think he was an idiot.

"What are you apologizing for?" Rec laughed, leaning their foreheads together. "Just relax and enjoy it, eh? We're enjoying each other's bodies. This is supposed to be good."

"Feels like everything's different these days," he admitted.

"Well, I bet a blow job still feels pretty damn good." Rec slid off the couch onto his knees.

It took Barclay a second to realize exactly what Rec's change of position meant. When it dawned on him, he was floored. "I…. Oh. You mean it?"

Rec smiled up at him and grabbed the waistband of his sweats, tugging on them. "It would be really mean to tease about this."

"Yeah. Yeah, it totally would." He managed to raise his ass up the tiniest bit, and he hoped it was enough to help.

Sure enough, Rec got his sweatpants down. Barclay's erection caught on them for a moment before Rec wrapped a hand around his cock and fished it out. Another hand job would have been just fine, but he sure wasn't going to complain about getting more than that. Not for a second.

Rec licked the tip of his cock, tongue flat and sliding around it like it was an ice cream.

Barclay's eyelids fell to half-mast, his balls drawing up tight. He curled his fingers into fists, and the only reason why he remembered to breathe was because he moaned and that took air.

"Don't come too fast—I want you to enjoy it." Rec licked again, tongue lingering on his flesh.

"I'll try not to." He curled his toes this time, squeezing them tight.

Rec gave him a cheeky grin. "Actually, you come as soon as you need to." With that, Rec opened up and took the whole head of Barclay's cock in, lips wrapping around the ridge beneath the crown.

"Thank you. I want…. This is so good." He wasn't sure how he'd managed to get any words out, but he thought he was at least semicoherent. He didn't really care if he wasn't.

Rec hummed and slapped the top of Barclay's cock, tongue working his slit for a moment, pressing into it, and slapping against it again.

"Rec!" Barclay's eyes crossed, his heart skipping a beat. Not just the first blow job he'd had in forever, it was gearing up to being the best one. Ever.

Rec slapped his cockhead again. Then the suction began, slow and steady.

No one had ever sucked him like this, like they loved it. It went on too, Rec changing it up now and then, sometimes sucking hard, sometimes gently. There was a look of pleasure on Rec's face, his eyes closed like he was concentrating on experiencing it as much as giving it. Rec continued to use his tongue, focusing on Barclay's slit.

He cried out over and over, the burn and sting making his toes and fingers curl as the sensations built.

Then Rec increased his suction and bobbed his head, taking more of Barclay's cock in. Barclay started babbling; he couldn't hold it in. He didn't even try. He had no clue what he was talking about—it could have been anything, although it was probably nothing.

Rec hummed around his flesh, the sound encouraging, and continued sucking and taking more and more of his cock in. Without any warning, Rec got a hand between his legs and pushed gently at his balls.

Barclay shot, his entire body going tight and hard, his universe shattering. Rec swallowed, which meant he kept sucking as Barclay's orgasm went through him, and then it extended things, bringing several amazing aftershocks with it.

Barclay was going to die. Just expire from pleasure. He thought as ways to die went, this one was pretty damn good.

When Rec was done, he didn't simply pull off but took his time licking Barclay clean. It was almost like a mini–blow job in and of itself.

"You. Damn. I never. Not like that. Not at all." He felt like his eyes were too big for his sockets and his skin would never fit right again.

Rec gave the tip of his cock one more lick, then looked up at him. "You've never had a blow job before?"

"Not like that."

"There are other kinds?" Rec asked, a quizzical expression on his face. It sounded like a serious question, though, rather than a jibe.

"I guess not. Just being goofy." *Way to be suave, Barclay.*

"Or trying to compliment me on my technique, which I only just now twigged to." Rec made a face. "I'm a dork. But I really enjoy having a nice cock in my mouth…."

"It shows. That rocks. You rocked. Thank you." Barclay was so wonderfully melted, he wasn't sure he'd ever be able to move again.

Rec rubbed his cheek against Barclay's cock, a hint of roughness from his stubble making Barclay shiver. "You're welcome." Rec climbed back up to sit next to him again, an obvious bulge in his shorts.

"Do you want…? I won't leave you hanging." He wasn't a dick like that.

"I'm not going to say no to a little help with my stiffie." Rec laughed. "You want me to pull my shorts down?"

"Yeah. Please." Barclay reached out for the heavy cock again, the weight more familiar this time. Rec had a good-sized prick, nice and thick, heavy with blood. The tip glistened from drops of precome, several of which he drew out as he slowly worked the length.

Rec's moan was sweet music to his ears. Shifting slightly, Rec looked at him, a soft smile on his face. "Your fingers feel great."

"If you come up here, I can suck you. I'm not sure I can bend over." He suddenly very much wanted to return the favor. He wasn't nearly as good at it as Rec was, but he was pretty sure there was no such thing as a bad blow job. Unless you used teeth. He knew that from bitter experience. He shook the thoughts from his head and concentrated on Rec.

"I'll make it work." Rec gave him an eager grin and stood. Rec tugged his shorts right off, then climbed onto the couch, planting a foot on either side of Barclay. That put the thick cock pretty much at mouth height.

"Oh…." Perfect. And yum. The glistening head was right there, offered to him. Barclay opened up, tongue sliding around Rec's cockhead.

Rec groaned and put a hand on Barclay's shoulder, fingers curling in. He thought maybe Rec would start fucking his mouth, and he wasn't sure how he felt about that. He really wanted a chance to do this blow job right, and for it to be a blow job, not a mouth-fucking. At least not to start with. Rec didn't fuck his mouth, though. Instead, Rec let Barclay have total control.

He moaned softly, then began to suck, bobbing his head nice and slowly. Rec groaned for him, free hand dropping to his head to stroke through his hair. That connection felt good, like he was more than just a convenient hot hole for Rec's dick.

Barclay slid his hands up the backs of Rec's thighs and found Rec's ass. He cupped it and held on. It felt damn good in his hands.

"That's it, baby. So good. Suck me." Rec's words tumbled down over Barclay, pleasing him.

He relaxed back, his moans muffled by the hardness between his lips. Rec began to rock gently, but it was enough to send the thick heat across Barclay's tongue, and he encouraged the thrusts to go deeper now, encouraged Rec to push harder. The sweet words and easy pace made him feel like he was still in control of the blow job.

Rec's words stopped, replaced by heartfelt groans and low moans as Rec thrust faster, cockhead going deeper. Barclay swallowed hard over and over, begging for more. He'd never felt cherished while giving a blow job before. Rec was turning the day into a whole lot of extremely enjoyable firsts.

Rec gave him more, fucking his mouth, giving him every inch. Finally he tugged Rec in deep, swallowing over and over and demanding Rec's orgasm. He wanted to taste Rec's spunk, but he needed to get Rec off, to be the one to do that.

"B!" Rec's shout filled the room as his come filled Barclay's mouth, pouring out of Rec. Barclay swallowed hard again and again, taking in every single drop.

Rec's hair-petting slowed, and he slid his hand down to cup Barclay's cheek, thumb touching where his mouth met Rec's cock. "Such a pretty, talented mouth."

The words made him moan, made his cheeks burn.

Rec pulled back slowly, and Barclay squeezed the velvety flesh with his lips, trying to keep Rec in a moment longer. Rec's cock left his lips with an audible pop that had Barclay's cheeks heating further, but Rec didn't seem concerned as he carefully stepped off the couch and tugged up his shorts before sitting down next to Barclay, leaning hard.

"You taste good, man," Barclay whispered.

Smiling, Rec leaned in and kissed him, lips lingering as he slipped his tongue into his Barclay's mouth. Rec broke the kiss long enough to tell him, "I taste good in your mouth."

Oh. Oh, that was… so good. Barclay opened up his mouth, his eyes closing. Rec deepened the kiss, but it was sloppy, almost lazy.

He could go with that—lazy and easy, sloppy and warm. The kisses went on and on, Rec seeming as happy as he was to do nothing more than kiss. It was wonderful to have this, someone who wanted to do more than simply get off with him.

The buzzer going off broke them apart. Rec grinned sheepishly. "That's gotta be our pizza."

"Yeah. Yeah, that went fast." The time had zoomed by and had been the most fun he'd had in eons.

"Yeah." Rec made sure he was presentable and went over to the intercom by the door to buzz the pizza guy up.

Barclay stayed where he was, watching as Rec opened the door and lounged there. He hadn't had pizza since he'd left his folks—it was a pain in the ass to have to worry about getting to the door. It was far easier to make himself a bowl of cereal. So this was going to be a real treat.

Barclay could barely see the delivery guy when he showed up at the door, and he couldn't hear anything as the guy and Rec chatted. It wasn't long before Rec shut the door and came back to the couch with two pizza boxes, plus a bag with what had to be extras. The greasy smell hit Barclay right away and made him even hungrier than he had been.

"God, that smells good. Seriously." Like a slice of heaven.

"Yeah, like something really bad for us that we're going to eat anyway because it tastes so good." Rec laughed as he opened both pizza boxes, the amazing smells getting stronger. Then he opened the container with the wings and grabbed two ginger ales out of the bag. "Ta-da! Supper."

"Wow, what do I owe you?" He had a couple bills in his wallet.

"I invited you over, went and got you, then made you stay. It's my treat." Rec grabbed a slice of meatlovers and bit in, groaning as he took a bite.

"You sure?" He took a slice of his own. It looked so good.

"Yep. Eat. Enjoy. I'll work your ass off on Monday to make up for all the yummy calories."

"Yeah, yeah. I got a hollow leg." He'd never watched what he ate when he'd been working. He'd never even thought about it—just eaten whatever he wanted.

"Yeah? You one of those people who can eat their weight in fried foods and not gain a pound?"

"I sure hope so. I mean, so far...." He shrugged. It wasn't like he was watching what he ate now. He had no appetite.

"Lucky bastard." Rec laughed and rubbed shoulders with him.

"Yeah. It's all genetics."

Rec nodded sagely. "That's what I tell my clients all the time. It makes a difference. Makes a difference in what you need to do to bulk up or lose weight or whatever. Some people can eat what they want without consequences. Others have to work a lot harder not to put on weight." Rec shrugged. "We're all different."

"I just need to get back to work." Barclay was going slowly crazy stuck in his tiny apartment with nothing to do all day. Of course, he wasn't there now, was he? He needed to shake it off and enjoy this right here.

"It'll happen. You need to be patient. I know that's hard to hear when it's already been as long as it has, but trust me. In the end, it'll be worth it."

"I hope so. I have a shelf life." He wasn't getting younger, and eventually he wouldn't be able to keep doing the work. Some guys managed to make the transition from stuntman to stunt coordinator, but there were a lot more of the former than the latter.

"If you stay nimble, it'll be longer than you think," Rec told him.

"Yeah." He didn't know. Right now he was going to get his head out of his ass and eat pizza and breathe.

Rec turned the volume up a little on the movie that they'd managed to miss a good portion of at this point, and they sat companionably, munching on their pizza and the wings.

It was good to have company, to be with someone who liked him, who was easy to be with.

They finished the meatlovers between them, and then Rec opened the other one, which was chicken and mushrooms and onions with a white sauce instead of the red sauce. "Sorry, I should have mentioned they were different at the start—we could have had a couple pieces from each. Now I don't know if I have enough room for a piece of this one on top of the wings." Rec gave him a quick grin. "Good thing pizza tastes great cold."

"It totally does. Cold pizza is the breakfast of champions." Not that he would be here come morning, and he could hardly ask to take slices home with him—he hadn't paid for any of it in the first place.

"Yeah, it probably is. Still…." Rec grabbed one of the smaller pieces from the chicken pizza box. "You want a little one too?"

"Sure. Why not?" He was going to look like a python that had swallowed a water buffalo, but what the hell. It was delicious and beat cereal for supper, hands down.

Rec handed over a piece before grabbing the bag and pulling out another takeout container, this one full of little powdered doughnuts. "I remembered you like them."

"Oh. Oh wow." That was so kind—and a little amazing— that Rec had remembered and made the effort to order them. All of a sudden, Barclay wanted to know what it would taste like, licking sugar off Rec's lips.

Rec beamed. "You're easy to please—I like it."

"Thanks. I appreciate it." He totally did. Rec was the nicest guy.

Rec slid a hand along Barclay's thigh, the touch warm, friendly. More than that, it felt amazing. Barclay spread a little, his hips relaxing under the light touches. Oh wow. That was all it took for the pain that had begun to sit there right at the surface to back off, which was even better than the pizza.

Rec gave him a lazy but warm smile. "I'm having a great day, B. I hope you are too."

"I am. I'm glad you didn't let me cancel." This beat lying in bed all day feeling down and sorry for himself by a thousand percent.

Rec chuckled. "So it's a good thing I'm a pushy bastard."

"Especially up that hill, yeah."

The soft chuckles turned into full-out laughter, and Barclay thought he could get used to that sound. He really could.

He reached out, stroking the ridges of Rec's abs. Rec's laughter faded, and he took in a deep breath, looking at Barclay. "Feels good, B."

"Yeah?" He liked touching. He really liked touching Rec. The skin beneath his fingers was soft and warm, the six-pack gorgeous to look at too.

"Yeah. You got good hands. I like 'em on me." Rec put his own hand on top of Barclay's and stroked for a moment. Such a simple touch, but it felt really good, reinforcing Rec's words.

"Thank you for today." Barclay would never have imagined the invitation to watch movies could have turned into this.

"It was my pleasure." Rec leaned in and gave him a soft kiss. Then Rec grabbed the box of powdered doughnuts and offered him one, holding it up to his lips.

He opened instinctively, letting Rec feed him. The doughnut was sweet and cakey and utterly delicious.

"You next." He wanted that kiss. As good as the doughnut had been, it was licking the sweet from Rec's lips that he really wanted. That he craved. He wasn't sure how he could crave something he'd never had before, but he did.

Rec offered him the box so he could grab one to feed to Rec.

"Oh." Hell yeah. He picked the best one he could find and offered it over, holding the treat up to Rec's mouth.

Rec took a bite from it, powdered sugar going all over his lips just like Barclay had envisioned.

He licked his own lips, his gaze glued to Rec's sweet-covered mouth. "I want to kiss you again. Can I?"

"I'd love that." Rec leaned in closer, eyes on Barclay's lips now.

"I would too." He moaned, tracing Rec's lips with the tip of his tongue, sampling the sugar.

Rec opened his mouth, tongue slipping out to touch his.

"Sweet." Barclay moaned and pressed their lips together, taking the kiss he'd wanted. There was still residual sugar on Rec's lips, and it made the kiss everything he could have hoped for.

Rec smiled and slid a hand behind his head, cupping his scalp and deepening the kiss.

It wasn't going to go anywhere, but it didn't have to. This time it could just be tasting. Rec hummed, the sound pleased, happy. They licked each other's lips and sucked on each other's tongues. The sugar made everything a little heady, a little wonderful. He didn't know if doughnuts would ever taste as good again if they weren't accompanied by the flavor of Rec's lips.

"Mmm. God, you taste way better than the food." Rec's words echoed his own thoughts so well it was almost like Rec was reading his mind.

Then Rec shifted, straddling him and cupping his face. Rec brought their mouths back together, and this time the kisses felt like Rec was trying to devour him. He approved. In fact, he loved it. He felt real for the first time in months.

Rec wasn't putting a lot of weight on him, but he could feel the heat of Rec's body washing over him. It felt safe, comfortable. Right.

Rec leaned away for a moment, reached back and came up with another doughnut. He put it between their mouths, the sugar sweet and immediately melting on Barclay's lips.

So decadent. Decadent and weird and wonderful all at the same time.

They each ate from their own sides, and while it was somewhat awkward, it was fun and sexy too. When they'd eaten all the treat away, their lips met in the middle, sugar and crumbs coating them. Rec licked Barclay's lips clean and sucked on the lower one.

"Crazy." This was mad fun. Seriously.

"Crazy delicious." Rec noted. "I could eat you right up."

"And we've already done that," he teased. He felt light and happy, almost giddy.

"Yeah. That's how I know you taste better than any doughnuts ever." Rec licked his lips like he was remembering the flavor of Barclay's come on them.

Barclay laughed, wrapped his hands around Rec's ass, and held on. Rec pushed back into the touch, then forward, bringing their cocks together. Rec rubbed, hips moving in circles to mash their covered pricks against each other.

He didn't have a third in him, did he? Did it matter? As Rec kept kissing him, rocking gently against him, he didn't think it mattered.

They were kissing and rocking and touching, and it felt so good. He wanted to sink into it and luxuriate in the sensations.

Rec didn't seem to be in any hurry or wanting to stop, so Barclay went with it and enjoyed everything about it. He didn't want it to end, and he had a hunch Rec didn't either. Still, it was getting late.

"If I don't go soon, I'll miss the last bus," he warned, just in case.

Rec made no move to get off him or back off in any way. "Honey, my bed is more than big enough for two."

Happiness flooded through him at Rec's words. "Just wanted to give you the option."

"What kind of idiot has the kind of day we've had and sends you home with the last bus?"

"A big one, I guess." And that made him pull Rec down for another kiss—just because.

Rec followed that up with yet another kiss and then another, pushing the worry about buses totally out of his mind. He had a safe place to stay, a warm body to stay with, and cold pizza for breakfast.

It didn't get much better than that.

Chapter Four

REC WOKE up early, like he always did. Today he was spooned up behind a warm body. Which he did not always do.

B.

Humming happily, he pressed closer, his morning wood sliding against Barclay's ass. It had been too long since he'd woken up with someone in his bed. He'd almost forgotten how nice it was.

Barclay moaned softly for him and arched, rubbing right back, that pert little ass moving against his cock and hips.

God, Barclay was sensual. Sexual. Rec wanted to fuck him into the mattress. He settled for nibbling on Barclay's neck to start with. He didn't use his teeth, just his lips, slightly parted so he could slip his tongue out to taste.

Someone obviously liked that. Barclay arched against him, sweet and slow. Rec hummed and rubbed harder. He wanted inside Barclay's lovely body, but he'd settle for rubbing off together.

Barclay's moans filled the air, the sounds moving from asleep to aroused as he moved.

"Morning." Rec licked Barclay's ear, loving the way he shivered in response.

"Hey. Hey, good morning." Barclay sounded part sleepy, part surprised, and definitely part aroused.

"Anything hurting?" Rec was totally up for some good solid massage where needed to knock any pain on its ass. That was more important than getting off.

"Just the normal aches leftover from the fall."

"You want a massage for that? Or something more for this?" He slid his hand down Barclay's body, wrapping his fingers around the half-hard cock he found and rubbing his thumb across Barclay's cockhead.

"Oh…. Oh." That was a wonderful, needy sound. "That feels so good."

"Perfect. It's supposed to." Rec ran his nose along Barclay's neck and hummed, then licked. God, he was already addicted to Barclay. To the taste of him, to the feeling of him, to the scent of him here in the bedroom.

Barclay cuddled into Rec, his cock filling Rec's fingers. He kept rubbing his own need along Barclay's crack as he stroked the lovely prick. The heat in his hand was delicious, and he closed his eyes, enjoying it thoroughly.

"Mmm. I'm going to touch you everywhere." Barclay said it like it was a warning, but Rec was going to take it as a promise.

"Yes, please do." He wanted those touches, wanted Barclay to explore him completely. Every nook and cranny. And then he wanted to return the favor.

Barclay reached back, hand on his hip sliding on his skin. He swore he could feel tingles wherever Barclay touched. He hummed at the warmth and jacked Barclay faster.

Barclay rubbed against him, bucking against his cock. Rec groaned. "Gonna make me come, B." He was going to shoot right up Barclay's back if this continued much longer.

"You want... you want to fuck me?" Barclay asked. "Do you do that?"

God yes, he wanted to. "I'd love to fuck you. Do *you* do that?" He hoped so. He wanted Barclay very badly.

"I totally do that. At least I used to. I think I still can."

"I'd love to help you find out." Rec turned Barclay in his arms, admiring the slender limbs. Barclay was beautiful, and he turned Rec on.

Barclay met his gaze. "I'm ready to try."

"Then that's all we need." He considered for a moment. "Well, that and lube and a condom."

"Right. Do you have those?" Barclay asked, looking hopeful.

He smiled. "It just so happens I do. Don't move, I'll be right back."

"I can do that." Barclay grinned, winked, playing with him.

He laughed and kissed Barclay, then popped out of bed and went to the bathroom where he kept his supplies. Tube of lube and a box of condoms. He grabbed a couple of condoms out of the box. Just in case more than one was needed for any reason.

He wanted in, wanted to make Barclay come on his cock. His prick stayed nice and hard at the thought. And it bounced along in front of him as he went back to the bedroom. It made him grin, and he was still smiling as he returned to Barclay.

Barclay was stretched out, bones popping and creaking as he arched. Rec watched for a long moment from the doorway, admiring the naked man in his bed—slender limbs, the pretty belly, and the tousled hair. Then he walked in.

"Found 'em." He waved his lube- and condom-laden hands in the air.

"Good. I was stretching out the kinks." Barclay settled back.

"Oh, don't do that. I like the kink," he teased as he climbed back onto the bed.

Barclay chuckled softly. "I'm not sure I have any kink."

No kink? A man who did what Barclay did for a living wasn't into kink? That surprised him. "Are you sure?"

"No." Barclay shrugged. "I never worried about it much."

"There's so many fun things to explore." Rec laughed and lay down on top of Barclay, making sure he kept most of his weight on his arms. He didn't want to put any pressure on Barclay's limbs.

"Uh-huh. Exploring is good with me." Barclay sounded eager for it.

"Yeah?" He pressed kisses over Barclay's face, licked one cheek, both lips.

Barclay laughed softly, chasing Rec's lips. It made him smile and place more kisses, making these slow and easy. He rubbed their cheeks together, one side and then the other. He didn't feel any need to rush, and there was a freedom in that he enjoyed.

"Oh…," Barclay sighed, the man obviously starving for touch. Rec was aiming to be the one to feed that strong need.

He slid his fingers across Barclay's belly, feeling the hint of what had obviously been—and would be again—great abs. Barclay's core was still fairly solid. What Barclay needed was his flexibility back, his strength.

Rec would help him get that. Later. Right now, Rec was going to touch Barclay everywhere, then make love to him. He couldn't think of a better way to start a Sunday morning. In fact, right now he couldn't think of anything better, full stop.

Humming happily, he kissed Barclay and slowly slid his fingers from belly to nipples. He touched each one lightly, then went back to rub a little harder against them. They tightened up, calling to him, begging for more. He loved the way the scarring on the left made them different. It gave them personality.

He remembered that they were fairly sensitive too, and rubbed them between his thumbs and forefingers, pinching alternately. He found the scarring on the one nipple fascinating. He wanted to lick it, bite it, taste it, over and over.

Moaning, he went for it with his mouth, using the tip of his tongue to trace the old injury. Barclay whimpered softly, the sound so fucking hot. Rec pressed his mouth against Barclay's skin and hummed again.

"Please. So good." Barclay begged so prettily.

Rec moved to the other nipple and began to suck, tongue flicking back and forth across the tip of the hard little nub. It was so easy to start biting, tugging, giving Barclay a little more. Barclay gasped at that, body arching up toward his mouth. Needy. He approved. Hell, he more than approved.

The things he could do with this sensitive, needy man. Groaning at the thought, he rolled his body against Barclay's, wanting more contact.

"Yeah. I want you." Barclay hummed, rocking up to slide them together.

"God yes, me too." He grabbed the lube and slicked his fingers up. Then he got distracted feeling up Barclay's cock. He let his fingers wander over the hot flesh, exploring each ridge and vein. He squeezed, enjoying the spongy hardness.

Barclay sang for him, happy, needy little cries that made his eyes cross. He coaxed more of them out with his fingertips, pressing them into Barclay's slit. When he pushed deep enough that it would sting, Barclay arched, crying out. So he did it again, then again. He loved the way Barclay moved, the slender limbs graceful despite Barclay's injuries. And he was so beautifully responsive.

"Oh fuck. Please. That—that aches." Barclay's voice was painted by his need, soft and wanton.

"Please more? Because the ache is good and you want more and you want it over at the same time?" Rec asked. He wanted to hear Barclay say it. Wanted to hear him expressing his need.

"I—" Barclay shook his head, then nodded, then just pushed back against him.

He had to admit, that confusion was sexy as hell; he thought that Barclay being new to knowing all the things he could have, to knowing what he wanted, made him even more interesting.

Barclay shifted, rolling onto his side and rubbing his ass against Rec's cock. Barclay's offer was clear, sure, straightforward, and it made Rec happy that while Barclay might have no clue about kink, he did know what he wanted and wasn't afraid to ask for it.

Rec grabbed the lube again and slicked his fingers back up, getting them ready to push into Barclay's body. All the while he teased Barclay's slit with his other hand.

The next time that Barclay arched in his arms, he pushed a single finger into Barclay's ass, tight heat gripping him immediately. Damn, Barclay felt good inside, all silky heat.

"Oh." Barclay hummed, one leg falling in front of the other, giving Rec more room to maneuver.

"So nice and tight. You're gonna feel great around my cock." Rec didn't want to rush things, though. It had been a while for Barclay, and he was going to respect that. Besides, taking his time would only build anticipation and make it that much better when he finally sank into Barclay's body.

Barclay moaned for him, the sound deep and sweet as honey, so needy. Rec tilted Barclay's head back, then licked at Barclay's lips. He took another kiss, tongue pushing into Barclay's mouth. Barclay opened right up, moaning for him, crying out for him.

He slid his finger deep, then tugged it out again. In no time he was fucking Barclay with it, working the tight hole with plenty of lube. Barclay's body didn't fight him, instead pulled him in deeper.

Groaning, Rec worked another finger in, spreading them both wide, turning them inside Barclay. He worked Barclay's channel, opening him for the invasion to come.

"Mmm…." Oh, eager, happy sounds. It sounded like Barclay was not only enjoying it, but reveling in what Rec was doing to prepare the tight body.

Rec grinned and repeated the motions of his fingers. He fucked Barclay again, just as slowly now that he had two fingers working the tight heat as he had when he'd used only the one.

"You an anal man, B? You like having my fingers inside you? Do you want more? A lot more?" He had some amazing dildos and plugs. He could entertain Barclay's ass for hours. Days. Weeks. He might have to go make some purchases to make that years.

"I—Yeah." Barclay's initial hesitation disappeared, and he went on confidently. "Yeah, I like it. I like being touched."

"It's been a long time since you've been touched, hasn't it?" He could tell; he could read it in every reaction. Okay, so he also knew because Barclay had said he hadn't even had an erection since the accident. But every reaction told him the same story, backed Barclay's words up. Barclay was starving for the contact they shared.

"Yeah. Yeah, too damn long."

"I'll take care of you, B. I'll make it good." He wanted Barclay to come back for more. He wanted Barclay to beg for more.

"I don't doubt it. You're… generous."

That was one of the nicest compliments anyone had ever given him. Rec rubbed their cheeks together. "I want you to feel good. If that makes me generous, then so I am." He wasn't doing it to be generous, just to make Barclay feel good.

"You so are. I appreciate it." Barclay reached back and took Rec's cock, stroking it base to tip.

Amazing. It hadn't been as long for him as it had Barclay, but he was still hungry for Barclay's fingers on him, making him *feel*. He hummed and slid yet another finger into Barclay's hole, spreading the tight body wider.

Barclay tried to arch and open more, the motion a little stiff, a little awkward. Rec didn't want that. This was supposed to make Barclay feel good, not leave him with aching—or worse—muscles.

"How about we get you on your back with pillows under your legs?" he suggested. They could shift things around until Barclay was perfectly supported.

"I—I'm okay. I don't want it to be weird."

"You being comfortable isn't weird. It's... comfortable." Like Barclay straining his muscles and ending up in pain wouldn't be weird. Rec slid his fingers out of Barclay and grabbed a couple of pillows. He got Barclay situated comfortably and ran his hands along the man's inner thighs, starting above his knees and working upward to the point where they met Barclay's torso. Rec kept his touch fairly light.

"Oh." Barclay's eyes crossed.

Rec grinned. He'd thought "weird" would disappear under the weight of pleasure. He did it again, pressing more firmly this time. Then he rubbed with his thumbs, digging in, massaging deeply.

Groaning, Barclay bucked for him, trying to move toward his touches. That didn't look particularly comfortable, and he touched Barclay's belly, pushing gently down toward the mattress.

"Easy. Easy, I have you." Rec didn't want Barclay hurting himself. This was supposed to be all about pleasure.

"I know. I'm sorry. I am."

"Shh. No apologies." This wasn't about guilt or worries either. Rec kissed Barclay's belly, then looked up the lovely chest to his face. "You just need to lie back and enjoy it, okay?"

Barclay shook his head and sighed softly. "I'm not a lazy lover, you know."

"That's what you're worried about, B? Come on—I know you're on the injury list, and I don't expect you to be the perfect lover."

"I hadn't expected to be a lover at all," Barclay admitted.

"I'm glad you are. I'm enjoying myself. Are you?" He drew his fingers up along the insides of Barclay's thighs again, spreading them to get more coverage.

"Uh. Uh-huh. A lot." Barclay grinned at him, but the look was surprisingly young, worried.

"Excellent. That's what I was going for." Bending, he gave Barclay's belly another kiss, lingering this time. The sweet muscles rippled and jerked for him. Barclay was so wonderfully responsive.

Leaning over Barclay and feeding him one kiss after another, Rec slowly worked his fingers back into Barclay's hole. The tight little ring opened for him, begging him and welcoming him in. Barclay was still slick from his earlier prep, but Rec got some more lube and pushed it in.

It wouldn't be long now before Barclay was ready for him. He spread his fingers wide, tugged them partway out, then pushed in again. He loved the heat of Barclay's body and how it held his fingers tight. How it proved Barclay wanted him.

"You… you like to take your time." Barclay watched him with wide eyes, pupils huge.

"I like lazy Sunday morning fucks," Rec admitted. "And a first time with you—I want to make it special. I want you to remember me. Remember this." He wanted to be the best lover Barclay had ever had.

"I couldn't forget. No way." Barclay reached for him, hands smoothing down his chest. "I'm glad you asked me to come."

"I'm even more glad I came and got you." He gave Barclay a wink.

"Yeah. Yeah, me too." Barclay found his cock, fingertip sliding on his flesh. Fuck, that was good. Really good.

He moaned as Barclay wrapped those warm fingers around him. It was even better than the random touches, maybe even too good. "Not too much. I want to come inside you." He didn't want Barclay to stop, but he didn't want to pop off either, which enthusiastic stroking would result in.

"Easy. I get you." Barclay's touches gentled, became caresses instead of strokes.

"Mmm. Yeah, you do." He matched the movement of his fingers inside Barclay to the caressing of his cock, bringing them in sync. Barclay's eyelids went heavy, and the air buzzed with electricity.

Rec held on as long as he could, but finally he needed inside Barclay. He tugged his fingers away and grabbed a condom. "It's time, baby. I need to feel you come on my cock."

Barclay moaned for him, legs spreading a little wider. He ran his hand along Barclay's thigh—while he appreciated the gesture, he didn't want Barclay hurting himself.

"Let me do the work, hmm? You relax and feel."

Barclay immediately relaxed for him, and he smiled. Rec did enjoy how a sub gave himself over to a Dom, offering himself, his trust. Bending, he put a kiss on Barclay's belly.

Barclay gasped softly, moaning for him. Oh pretty.

He added lube to the condom and settled between Barclay's legs. "You ready, B?"

"I am. I'm open for you."

"You are." He pressed against Barclay's hole and added pressure until the head of his cock breached Barclay. He popped inside, the scrape and burn making his toes curl.

Barclay moaned for him, and he wanted to hear more. Much more. He slowly pushed the rest of the way inside, sinking all the way in. Fuck, he fit so good. Barclay was so fucking tight.

He met Barclay's gaze, held it as he stayed buried deep, panted as he let Barclay feel how well he fit.

"Full. God, you're big. Feels good."

"You do too." He circled his hips, moving his cock inside Barclay's body, jonesing on the dark flush that climbed up Barclay's belly.

He took a few more breaths, then began to pull out. Slowly. He was going to make this last. He was going to give Barclay the chance to experience every inch of this, every second of it. He felt the drag of B's tight little hole, begging him to stay in, to come back. He ignored that plea until only the tip of his cock remained inside Barclay, and then he pushed back in again, still slowly, carefully.

The pressure made him gasp, the squeeze around his cock enough to make his eyes cross.

"Fuck. You are perfectly tight." Honestly, it was like Barclay had been made for him, for this very purpose.

"Don't stop yet, please." Barclay begged so prettily.

"Oh no. Not yet. Not for as long as we can make it last." He could make it last a pretty long time.

Barclay nodded for Rec, moaning deep in his chest as they joined together. Taking it as a sign that Barclay was ready for more, Rec moved faster, taking Barclay over and over, forcing them to grind together as he dove in.

He pressed their mouths together, tongue-fucking Barclay, the motions echoing his hips. The way he leaned made his cock shift, made Barclay arch hard.

Rec stayed there, loving the way it made Barclay move and moan. He drove in with short, sharp jerks, trying to peg Barclay's gland. Barclay began crying out and trying to move into his thrusts. Bingo.

He growled and kept it up, needing Barclay to fly. He found a pace where he could keep pounding in without tiring out too quickly, caught between wanting this to go on forever and wanting to push them both over the edge.

Not wanting Barclay getting stiff, though, he drove harder and wrapped his hand around Barclay's cock. He dragged his fingers along the turgid flesh.

Barclay moaned and held on, begging him for more, harder, deeper. He gave it all, humping harder into Barclay's body.

Barclay grabbed his own cock, tugging himself off.

"When I say. We'll do it together."

"Uh-huh." Barclay nodded, pulling harder.

"On three. One. Two. Three." He slammed in hard, freezing while deep, and came.

Barclay worked his tip once, hard, and shot, following right behind him. The way Barclay's body squeezed him milked several aftershocks out of him, and he collapsed, trying hard to keep most of his weight off Barclay.

"Good... good morning," Barclay groaned.

That made him chuckle, and he rubbed their noses together. "Good morning. Very good morning."

"Uh-huh. Best morning in... forever."

"Glad to be a part of that!" Rec smiled as he held the base of the condom and pulled out of Barclay. He took a moment to dispose of the condom, then came back to cuddle with Barclay, taking the lean body into his arms.

Barclay moaned softly, then cuddled in.

"You hungry?" He had Eggos in the freezer and syrup in the cupboard. He could do bacon too.

"I'm cool right this second."

"Yeah, me too," he admitted. He did love the aftercare. Even if it was just cuddling.

Barclay kissed his cheek, his jaw, the connection gentle. Humming, Rec brought their mouths together, no tongue or big devouring, just a gentle buss to match Barclay's. Barclay leaned into him with a sigh.

"Wow, huh?" Barclay's words were soft, almost lazy.

"Yeah. That was yum. You were yum."

"We're pretty yum."

Rec laughed and started singing, "I'm a yum, he's a yum, wouldn't you like to be a yu-um too?" The old commercial ditty was now stuck in his head, he was sure.

Barclay's laughter filled the air, warm and happy.

Rec squeezed Barclay tight, happy as a clam in this moment. He kept touching, stroking randomly. "You going to stay today? Watch a couple more movies and hang out?"

"You want me to? I don't want to be a burden."

"Oh yeah, because sitting next to a sexy guy and having a blow job snuck between acts is such a hardship."

Barclay pinked and snuggled in, whispering in his ear. "Yesterday when I sucked you, when you rode my mouth? That was the sexiest thing ever."

"Yeah? I thought it was pretty fucking hot too—watching you take it."

Barclay shivered against him, the sensation utterly delicious. Was he one of those men who liked hearing dirty talk? Rec was pretty good at it.

"You have a mouth made for sucking, you know. Sweet and pink, hot as fire."

Barclay's cheeks went red, but he wriggled against Rec too, pushing toward him.

"Seriously, I can't wait to sink back into you, fill you up with my cock again. Your ass…."

"You don't have to flatter, you know. I don't expect it."

"It's not flattery, B. It's the truth." He ran his finger around the outside of Barclay's left nipple, and the little bit drew up tight. Watching it, he took it between two fingers and pinched lightly.

That earned him a soft gasp, and Barclay's hips rolled. "You're going to make me hard again, man."

"Mmm. I don't have a problem with that. Not at all." He let Barclay's nipple go, then flicked his tongue across it, just the once. "I like how they tighten up for me, how you want it. Your hard little nubs feel good in my fingers. They feel even better against my tongue."

"Jesus.... You.... I want you. Again. Crazy, huh?"

"I don't think it's crazy at all." He was taking it a compliment, in fact. He began to circle Barclay's other nipple.

He could make a morning of exploring those tight little nips. He wondered what Barclay would think of that? He obviously had enough kink in him to have gotten one pierced in the first place. "You play much?" He wanted to know who'd topped Barclay. Had he ever been in a Dom/sub relationship with a full-time lover? Or did he just dabble?

"Play?" Barclay looked honestly confused.

"The lifestyle? BDSM?" That's why Barclay had looked for a trainer at the Iron Eagle, right?

"I... I mean, I don't think I do that."

Well, he found that hard to believe. His gut told him Barclay was a sub, and his gut rarely lead him wrong. "I just assumed you would as you were at the Iron Eagle. It does cater to Doms and subs. I'm a Dom, by the way."

"I just.... Tide suggested it, said you could help me."

"He was right, I can. And the lifestyle's got nothing to do with it. I guess I just assumed you were a member of the gym and therefore a part of the community. How do you know Tide?" He stroked Barclay's back, seeking to soothe—he could sense Barclay starting to worry about the whole setup.

"We know each other through work. He models and I do too, and often we'll be at the same photo shoots, so we knew each other a bit. Then he saw me in a coffee shop in the chair. Like I said, we got to chatting and that's how you came up."

"Right. That makes sense." He gave Barclay a smile and rubbed their noses together. "I think you'd like the lifestyle."

"Lifestyle? You mean being gay or—"

"I mean the BDSM. Doms and subs, bottoms and tops." He wondered how much Barclay knew about it.

"Oh. That's cool. Hot, I mean. I mean, I don't do it, but... yeah."

"But if you think it's hot, you'd be into trying it out." He wasn't going to beat around the bush. He liked Barclay a lot, and if he had his druthers, they'd both be into the same things.

"Maybe. I mean, I don't know. I'm not, like, super sexy or anything."

"Says who? I think you're incredibly sexy. Honestly, I do."

"I'm not your typical guy, though."

He drew back and looked at Barclay. "What do you mean?"

"Like I'm skinny and all knobby knees and elbows. I'm made for parkour, not being sexy."

"You don't think parkour is sexy? Barclay, that's fucking sexy, trust me."

Barclay pinked, obviously pleased. "Thank you."

He had a hunch Barclay wouldn't appreciate being called a twink, even if it was meant as a compliment, so he didn't go there. "The gym has a ninja training area behind the building. Tide's boy trains on that."

"Yeah, I heard. So cool. I could have shredded that once upon a time."

"We'll get you there again." From the information Rec had, he could see no reason why Barclay couldn't expect a full recovery with time and work. Maybe it would never be as easy as it had been, but that was life. Just getting older did that to you. Drive and determination and hard work could overcome that.

He nuzzled Barclay's neck, breathing in the smell of man and sex. He liked Barclay's scent—he liked that their scents were mingling even more.

"Mmm. That's nice. For real."

He had to agree. "Yeah. I love that we've got time. This is what lazy Sundays are all about." Even if he was going to have to feed them eventually.

"Yeah. Yeah, this one's better than most."

"Best one I've had in I don't know how long." He kept touching and kissing, nuzzling. It honestly felt wonderful.

"Eons." Barclay nibbled his earlobe.

"Eons. F-ons. G-ons. H-ons." He started to laugh at that point and couldn't continue the joke.

"H-ons? Wow." Barclay actually bit him a little.

"Hey, it was a great joke. Fantastic even." He had to be in a good mood if he was pulling out the puns and wordplay.

"Great? Maybe okay." Barclay started tickling his ribs, and he hooted, wriggling to try and stay away from Barclay's fingers. "Careful—I will retaliate."

"Promises, promises!"

"Oh, it's like that, is it?" Laughing, Rec rolled up and over, straddling Barclay's hips. He managed to grab both of Barclay's wrists and tug them up over his head. Then he put both of Barclay's wrists into one hand and held them up over Barclay's head as he used his free hand to dig into Barclay's ribs.

He was gentle, but Barclay laughed regardless, cackling for him. He rolled them carefully, but was back up top by the time he'd stopped, holding Barclay as he kept enough of his weight up so he didn't crush his boy.

His boy.

Oh, he did like that thought.

He brought their mouths together, exploring whether or not Barclay tasted different now that he'd thought that. Barclay hummed for him, the sound soft and a little wondering. God, he could eat this man up.

"You taste so good "

"Thank you. This is… so unexpected. Wonderful, though."

"Thank you. I'm loving it too." And hopefully this was only the first morning of many they'd get to spend indulging in each other.

Time would tell.

Chapter Five

BARCLAY HEADED into the gym, rolling slowly. He'd had the most amazing weekend and it had totally sucked to get back to real life.

Still, Rec was waiting for training, and he'd get to see the man again. That was good.

Rec was at the counter, chatting to the kid behind the desk. The kid was laughing, eyes shining, looking at Rec like he'd hung the moon.

Oh. *Yeah, remember, there are guys in better shape that have way more access. Remember, you haven't made any promises.*

Rec glanced over, noticed him, and straightened right away, his face lighting up as he came toward Barclay. "There you are. And right on time too."

"Hey. Good afternoon." He had to smile back. Had to.

Rec touched his shoulder. "How are you doing?"

"Better now." Oh, that was a silly thing to say.

Rec looked pleased, though. "I know what you mean."

"Yeah? You… you ready to work out?"

"The question is are you?" Rec led him over to the machines, and he found himself noticing the way Rec's muscles moved under his tight shorts and T-shirt.

"Yeah. Yeah, time to work."

"Yeah, let's make you flexible again." Rec gave him a wink, and they started to work.

"I hope so. I want to be. I want out of this chair."

"Speaking of, let's get you out of it and onto the bench."

"Right." He grabbed for his crutches, but Rec shook his head.

"Grab me. I'll stabilize you."

He wasn't sure about that, but Rec was right there, making it happen, and suddenly he was on the bench, sitting pretty.

"Way to go. I'm going to start you at the same weight you were doing on Friday."

"Okay. I can do it." He was feeling strong.

"I know you can."

With that encouragement, he started working out, Rec spotting him and guiding him through one machine after the other. Rec did not go easy on him but didn't let him overdo, either, calling a halt to things earlier than he would have on his own. "You don't need to wear yourself out, baby. You have to work smart. If you wait until you're hurting to stop, you've waited too long."

Rec helped him back to his chair. "You want to shower? I'd be happy to help you out."

"Yeah, if you don't mind."

"I don't mind in the least. And unlike on Friday, I'm not going to promise not to ogle or touch this time. I mean, I can be strictly professional if you'd prefer."

"I think... I think that bird has flown, hmm?"

"Yeah, but I could pretend if you wanted me to." Rec's smile was warm, fond.

"I think that sounds less than fun," he admitted. "Unless of course you have another client and need to get to it."

"Nope. Just you today. And even if I pretended, I'd still be admiring your hot bod." Rec wheeled him into the showers and down to the big stall at the end of the row.

"This won't get you in trouble with your boss?"

"You mean showering with you?" Rec shook his head. "You noticed all the stalls were a little larger than at most gyms? That's so two can shower comfortably. Together. Like really together."

"No one minds? Really?" That was cool.

"God no. That's what this place was made for. Upstairs is a Doms' floor and a floor where couples can have sex, do scenes, turn working out into foreplay, etc. There's a sub area there too. It's totally built around the community's needs." Rec began to strip down. "Do you need help getting undressed?"

He wasn't sure half of that was English. "No, I can manage." Thank God he'd brought something to change into this time.

"Cool. There's a couple towels down here already, so we're good on that front. And I'll help you up and you can lean on me under the spray. There's a bench in here as well if that would be easier. I kind of like the idea of you leaning against me, though." Rec waggled his eyebrows comically, but the look in his eyes was warm, not jokey at all.

"Just don't let me fall, okay?" He didn't want to go down.

"I won't." Rec sounded very sure, and that confidence made him relax. Rec had this.

He stripped down, finding it easier this time. Rec had explored all his scars. He could feel Rec's eyes on him, see the admiration in them. So instead of making him more self-conscious, it made him feel... sexy. Sensual. Whole. He could get used to it.

Once he was naked, Rec came over and held out his hands. He took them, Rec pulling as he worked to stand, and it wound up being pretty smooth moving from the chair to standing against Rec's muscled body.

His own muscles didn't want to hold him up, his legs shaking, and he held on a little desperately.

"I've got you," Rec murmured, one arm across his back, the other along it, holding on to his ass. "Just lean against me."

"I'm sorry. I didn't think I'd be so weak."

"It's not weakness. You just worked out and your muscles are tired." Rec took a few steps back, bringing him into the hot spray.

He stopped holding himself up, the heat melting him straightaway. Rec remained steady, supporting him even as Rec let go of his ass and grabbed some soap, working it into suds against his skin. It smelled fresh and manly.

"Mmm. This feels good, Barclay, the way you're pressed against me."

His cheeks went warm.

"I like that you're willing to let me support you. That feels good too. Knowing you trust me." Rec's soapy fingers circled his asscheeks before slipping along his crack.

"Oh...." Oh, was this okay?

Rec rubbed their cheeks together, fingers slipping away, then back, sliding between them to find his cock and balls and running slowly over them too. It was slow and easy and sexy as hell.

"You're okay," Rec murmured. "Just relax and enjoy my touches."

"No one will care?" He wouldn't get Rec in trouble.

"I promise. Nobody will care." Rec turned them. "And now the only ass anyone'll see—if they look—is mine."

"I trust you." Rec knew the rules, right?

"I appreciate that, thank you." Rec kissed the top of his head and continued to move those soapy hands over him, half cleaning, half arousing him. It was probably the best shower he'd ever had in his life. There wasn't a part of him Rec hadn't touched. Not one part.

He was harder than ever too. Well, maybe not harder than Rec had made him over the weekend, but hard. Needy. God, he wanted like he was a teenager or something.

Rec didn't seem to mind, finding his cock and wrapping a hand around it, slowly stroking the entire length of him.

"Oh...." He blinked as his balls drew up.

"A nice orgasm will help relax you," Rec murmured, continuing to work him.

"Will it?" He blinked up. He wasn't going to say no.

"It totally will." Rec covered his mouth, tongue slipping between his lips. Between that and the hand around his cock, he was lost in sensation.

He arched and hummed, trusting Rec to hold him. Each touch, each kiss, sent him higher, made him feel like he was spinning. Rec moaned, tongue-fucking his mouth. He began to cry out, heedless of where he was.

Rec pushed him up against the wall, hand moving faster, insistently. "That's it, B, come for me."

"Please. Please, I.... Yes."

"Yeah. Do it." Rec pressed his thumb against the tip of Barclay's cock and rubbed at his slit lips.

Heat poured out of him, his cock throbbing and balls aching.

Rec groaned, the kiss going on even as Rec's hand slowed, drawing two lazy aftershocks out of him before stopping altogether.

"W-wow." He trembled all over, shaking like a leaf on a tree.

"You're good. I've got you." Rec's words filled him, and he believed them. He was safe exactly where he was.

Which wasn't something he usually thought about.

"Sorry. Sorry. God, that was amazing. Thank you."

"You're welcome. And no apologies. You have nothing to apologize for." Rec peppered his face with soft kisses.

He found himself chasing the kisses, moaning softly. Rec shifted them so that Rec leaned against the wall, supporting Barclay with his solid body. The water ran down Barclay's back, beating on his shoulders in the best way.

They sat on the shower seat, and he settled in Rec's lap.

He heard someone come in, soft giggles sounding, and he tensed, but Rec stroked his skin and said "Shh."

The giggles cut off suddenly, the sound of flesh hitting the tile unmistakable.

"Rec?" he whispered. What the hell?

"Someone else is 'enjoying' the showers like we did. We can either sneak past them and go to the locker room now or wait until we're alone again." Rec kept touching, stroking.

"Oh…."

"…going to beat your ass, boy, make it pink for me."

"That's a master with his boy. Spanking is big in the BDSM world. Sometimes it's used as punishment, but just as often it's not. It's very hot for both parties."

"Spread wide, boy, push yourself out toward me."

"Are you imagining what they're doing?" Rec asked, still whispering into his ear.

He didn't answer, but he was. He so was.

"Hot baby, with your plugged hole. Does it still burn? Are you feeling the weight?"

"Yes, Master."

Rec moaned softly, the sound seeming to vibrate inside him. "I love the sound of that word spoken with such devotion."

Slaps started ringing through the bath. "Count, boy. You've earned twenty and then ten to your hole."

"Master!"

"You want fifteen? Or ten with the crop?"

"Please, Master… yes to the crop." There was so much need in that voice.

Barclay hid his face in Rec's throat, swallowing hard.

"Then you count and I'll take the plug out, whip your hole with the crop." The man's voice got softer. "Then I'll put more ginger oil on your plug, boy. Make you wear it for another hour while I watch you."

There was nothing but a whimper as an answer, and then, after several long breaths, a very soft "Yes, please, Master. Thank you, Master."

Rec moaned again, rocking Barclay against him.

"Good boy. Count."

The spanking started, the soft moaned words following each blow, and Rec rubbed against him in time.

Barclay couldn't believe this was happening. He also couldn't believe how turned on he was.

"I want you. I want to fuck you in time," Rec moaned, lips right on his ear.

He muffled his cry in Rec's throat.

Rec's hips rocked, motion echoing the sounds and counts coming from the other stall. Each rock slid Rec's cock along his belly.

"Almost there, boy. Your ass is rosy."

"I'm almost there too. Can you feel me leaking on your belly?" Rec asked.

Barclay nodded and reached down to play with Rec's leaking slit.

Rec groaned for him, humping up harder. "Don't stop."

Another moan sounded close to them. "Please don't stop."

Rec smiled against his skin, then licked his ear, then sucked on his earlobe. He answered by pushing a little harder, working the tip.

He heard a low cry, then something heavy hitting the tile. "Spread your cheeks for me, boy, and beg me to whip your hole."

"Please, Master. Do it now. Please, whip me. Whip me hard!"

Barclay jumped at the sharp slap, slamming into Rec. Another moan sounded against his ear, and when the next sound came, Rec pulled him in this time, their bodies coming together deliberately.

What was this? Was this okay?

"Stop thinking, B. Just go with it."

"Uh-huh. Does it hurt?" he whispered.

"Yeah. But it also feels good. And you can hear it. How much he wants it and loves it." Rec tapped his hole and made him gasp. "Get ready. There we are at eight. Are you ready to come with me when he hits ten?"

"Oh God…." Again?

"I know you are." Yeah, Rec was right—he was. This man made him come more….

He nodded and gasped as the sobbed "Nine! Master, please!" sounded.

"One more and we can come," murmured Rec, humping up against him.

The last crack was loud, the cry following it even bigger. "Ten! Master!"

"Now!" growled Rec, and heat splashed against his belly, against his cock as Rec came. It was like the words and the heat drew his own orgasm from him, and to his utter shock he was coming, splashing up over his hand. "Good boy. So good."

The words made him a little dizzy.

Rec rubbed their cheeks together and it felt so good to rub gently against him.

"This seems like a wet dream," he whispered.

"It's definitely wet," Rec whispered back before chuckling.

He muffled his laughter in the curve of Rec's neck. Oh God. Funny.

Rec held on to him, keeping him firmly in Rec's lap as they listened to the ecstatic sounds coming from the other stall. It was pretty clear they were fucking now, and just as clear they were being happily enthusiastic about it.

Whoa. And also wow. Barclay didn't know what kind of place this was. It had seemed so normal.

Rec held him until the other men left the showers; then he turned their water off and grabbed a couple of towels. One Rec wrapped around him, then pulled the other around his own shoulders. Next Rec dried him, the touches careful.

"Thank you. I—" God, he didn't want to go home, but what else could he do?

"You're welcome. And also thank you. That was awesome." Rec helped him get back into his chair and rolled him toward the locker room. "Have you got any plans for the rest of the day?"

"No. You?" *Please say no.*

"Not yet. I was kind of hoping that we could hang out together."

"I'm into that. Sure. Yes." Please.

Rec beamed at him. "Awesome!"

They got to the locker room where two good-looking guys were getting dressed, one of them looking totally dazed. Oh God, it was the guys they'd been listening to.

He kept his eyes down, praying that his chair made him invisible. He'd noticed that, the way people tended to ignore him so much more down here.

The two men nodded at him and Rec, and the dazed guy gave them a blissed-out smile.

Rec chuckled and nodded back. "Good session, eh?"

"The best."

"Yeah. Here too. Have a nice day." Rec looked like butter wouldn't melt in his mouth.

"You too!" The guy who'd spoken to them tied his shoes, then offered the blissed-out guy a hand, hauled him up, and they left together arm in arm.

"That was…. Did they know we were there?"

"I don't think they cared one way or the other, to be honest." Rec grabbed his clothes and began putting them on.

"Oh." He would have cared, he thought. He wasn't sure if he'd be angry, but he thought he'd care.

"They were into each other and what they were doing, and they knew there might be people watching or listening, but they did it anyway. Hell, there's people here who are into being watched."

"Yeah? Cool…." He was beginning to be a little wigged.

"Come on. Get dressed and we'll figure out what to do with the rest of our day."

"Sure." He wanted to ask if he'd done okay, but that seemed like a weenie thing to do.

Rec was dressed quicker than he was but didn't try to hurry him along or offer to help. Instead he asked, "You got any questions?"

"Huh?" Oh, he had about a zillion, but he wasn't going to ask.

"I'd be happy to answer any questions if you have them. About the lifestyle. About anything, really. Life, the universe, and everything, you know?"

"I don't know what to ask. What… what do you want to do?"

"Well, we could do movies again—though we both know that'll probably just end in more blow jobs." Rec grinned. "We could go for a wander. We could go eat. We could play video games. I'm easy. I just want to spend time with you."

"I'm not hungry yet, but we could go to the park for a while, then see…."

"Sounds good. It's a nice day out, so it should be great."

"Yeah, it should, for sure."

"You ready?"

When he nodded, Rec took his hand. "Then let's go."

He held it for a minute, then grabbed his gloves. "Lead the way."

"Let me know if you need a push." Rec went to the front of the gym and held the door for Barclay.

"Will do. My arms will let me know about sex and workouts."

"Yeah, I bet they will. That's why you get tomorrow off the workout—it'll give your muscles the time they need to recover."

"Yeah. I'll spend a couple hours walking on my hands."

"Seriously? Or euphemistically?"

"I have in the past. I can't do it for a couple hours, but I can manage for thirty minutes, I think."

"No. I forbid it. You have to take a day off in between working out. But I tell you what—when you're back in tiptop shape, I am so challenging you to do that."

"Can you forbid it?" Was that a thing?

"I just did."

Well, he didn't know what to say to that, honestly, so he didn't say anything.

"Do you ever feel like you could have done better, that you might have chosen differently?"

"Huh? In what way?" He didn't understand.

"I don't know—like something is missing. Or that there could be more for you."

"Maybe? I don't know. I never thought I'd be like this."

"Be like what?"

"Broken. Living on a mattress on the floor." Hated. He'd never thought someone would hate him enough to want to kill him.

"You're not broken, B. I swear."

"Maybe seriously cracked."

"Well, if that's the case, we're going to glue you back together. I'm sorry it's been so bad, though." Rec really did sound sorry, as if he could have done anything about it.

"I'm cool. Seriously. I just have to get better."

"You'll get better." Rec chuckled. "Isn't that what they say? It gets better."

"Yeah. That's what they say."

They got to the park and headed along the path toward the center where there was a little pond.

"It's okay if you don't have faith yet—I'll have it for you."

"I'm not all hopeless and shit. I promise."

"I know. It's got to be hard to spend so much time out of commission, to know what your body used to be capable of, and now you're healing but it's so damn slow. I get it."

"Yeah. It was rough."

"Are you really worried you're not going to be able to make a comeback? And don't tell me you're not worried, because I can see that you are. Something's bothering you."

"It's no big thing." He didn't know how to tell the truth about what had happened. He couldn't.

"You sure? You just seem... I don't know. Maybe I'm reading into it."

"Don't worry. I'll wrestle my demons."

Rec gave him a long, measured look. "Maybe you don't have to wrestle them on your own. I know it's only been a few days, but I like to think we're friends now. With benefits at that. One of those benefits should be having someone you can talk to, talk things out with."

"I think we are too. Seriously. You've been... amazing." More than. Rec was like an angel.

"Ditto on the amazing." Rec squeezed his shoulder and helped him set his chair by a bench near the small pond. Trees shaded the area, and a breeze blew through. Sitting on the bench, Rec tilted his head back and closed his eyes for a moment. "Listen to those birds and bugs make noise."

"Crazy, isn't it? How this is so green in the middle of all this hustle and bustle?" He wished he could go run through the grass.

"Yeah. I love coming here. Most of my runs involve the park in some way."

"I used to run this one too." A long time ago.

"Then we'll have to go together when you're up to it again." Rec gave him a warm smile.

"Works for me." He could do that.

"I'm going to hold you to it, B." Rec took his hand and twined their fingers together.

He loved that, how Rec reached for him, held him. Their fingers fit damn well together too, like they were made for each other.

God, that was cheesy. And probably pretty damn presumptuous. Still, he could be ridiculous in his own head if he wanted to.

Rec squeezed his hand and gave him a rather goofy smile. Maybe it wasn't so presumptuous after all.

"It's a gorgeous day." Barclay didn't know what else to say.

"It is. I think a little sun will do you good. How are you feeling? Muscles feeling a little tired?"

"Yeah. You know, shaky."

"You ready for something to eat? That'll probably help. There's a hotdog cart on the south side of the park."

"Oh, that sounds good." He could totally deal with that.

"Awesome." Rec stood and went around to the back of his chair, unlocking the wheel before pushing him back onto the path. "What do you like on your wiener?"

"Chili and cheese. You?" He leaned back and winked.

"Well, I do like that special sauce." Rec waggled his eyebrows.

Barclay laughed happily, tickled deep down. "I do like my tube steak."

Rec's laughter joined his, and by the time they got to the hotdog stand, they were chortling like mad.

They ordered their hotdogs, breaking into chuckles whenever they stopped to breathe.

Once they'd paid and received their dogs, Rec pushed him back to a quiet bench and sat on it next to him. "Would it be weird if I sat and watched you eat?"

"You aren't hungry?"

"Yeah, but I can eat a hotdog anytime. Watching you eat is going to be special."

"Goof." Barclay's cheeks turned hot, but he focused on his dog, on getting the perfect bite.

"Mmm. Look at that mouth." The words were soft, barely spoken.

Oh God. Seriously? Oh God. He wriggled in his chair.

"Yeah, you make me feel like wriggling too."

"Eat your hotdog." Barclay tried to take another bite. He could feel Rec's eyes on him, though, watching every move he made, and suddenly he saw it, the way he was opening his mouth to get his lips around the bun.

God, this was perverse and heated and wonderful.

He glanced at Rec, found the man licking his lips, those eyes glued to him.

He licked chili off his lips. Damn.

Rec hummed. "So pretty. I could eat you up." It should have sounded cheesy, silly, but it didn't. It was hot, and the words went straight to his balls. Rec could make him want so quickly.

"I bet the hotdog is better." God, Rec was something.

"No way. I've had a taste of you—trust me, this dog's got nothing on yours." Rec took a bite of his hotdog, a blob of mustard left behind on the corner of his mouth.

"You have…." He leaned forward and caught the mustard on his finger, bringing it to his mouth.

Rec moaned for him, the sound resonating in his balls, and he swallowed hard. How had eating hotdogs in the park turned him hard and needy?

Barclay dropped his eyes and focused on his food. He was in public; he didn't do this sort of thing now. Anymore. Whatever.

When he looked up again, Rec was still watching him, although he'd finished his dog too. Rec smiled, and he smiled back automatically, feeling warm inside.

"You want to come back to my place? I've got something I want you to try."

"Sure. I like your place." It was comfortable and open enough for him to function.

"Thanks. I like it too. And it feels great to have you in it. I had this toy that was still in the box, and I set it up this morning. I was hoping you'd come by again today after our session," Rec admitted.

"A toy? Like a game?"

"A toy like a sex aid." Rec grinned and it was wolfish, all teeth and wickedness. "You want me to tell you or do you want to be surprised?"

A sex aid....

"I want you to tell me." He didn't know what to think, but the expression on Rec's face was eager.

"It's a sling. It'll hold you so that you aren't having any aches or pains at all, and I can adjust the height, so it's perfect for both of us. You'll be pleasantly surprised at how comfortable you'll feel in it."

"A sling?" He shook his head, confused. "You'll have to show me."

"I will. You're going to love it, trust me." Rec stood and went behind his chair, hands coming down on the handles. "May I?"

"Yes. Thanks." It meant a ton to be asked.

Rec pushed him back onto the path and toward Rec's place. It was a gorgeous day, and he was glad they'd gotten out into it, but he had to admit he was happy to be going back to Rec's. The man was an addiction.

"Why did you decide to become a trainer, Rec?"

"I ran out of money for university, and doing personal training seemed to fit my skills and was a way to make money—I did two years of sports therapy, and I liked it enough that I decided to stick with it instead of finishing school."

"Very cool. I never went." He was sort of... just a dude that could throw himself off a building.

"I'm not sure they've got schools for stuntmening. Is that a word?" Rec laughed at himself. "So what movies have you worked on?"

He rattled off a few. He'd only done a couple of high-budget movies, but he'd worked in Vancouver and in Los Angeles a number of times.

"Oh cool! Have you watched them? I was thinking we could, and I'll see if I can figure out what parts you did. Or is that weird? Is it strange to watch yourself?" They turned onto Rec's block.

"You can't tell it's me. I'm just a body doing a trick."

"Oh. I mean even if you know what you're looking for? That's kind of disappointing."

"I mean, I know, but part of the job is to make it unnoticeable, right?"

"Yeah, I guess. But if you're the one I want to see, it's no fun that you can't tell." Rec dropped a kiss on the top of his head.

"I bet you can tell."

"I'd love to try. I like to think I'm getting to be an expert on your body." Rec opened the front door to his building and Barclay rolled himself in. It was considerably cooler in the lobby. They went to the elevator, and Rec pushed the button.

"I do love your elevator, Rec."

"It rocks, doesn't it? When I bought the place, I figured I could take the stairs for exercise, but I'll tell you what—I adored this thing with every box, every piece of furniture, when I moved in. And if I've got groceries—yay, elevator. If I had a long day at work—yay elevator."

Barclay began to laugh, the sound starting soft and then growing.

"You've got a great laugh, B. You should use it more often."

Funnily enough, he'd laughed more in the last few days with Rec than he had since he'd been hurt. "I agree. It feels so good to just be happy for a minute."

"Gonna try and make it longer than a minute. You deserve more."

The elevator dinged and Rec pushed him in.

Even though it was only the second time he'd been here, it was beginning to be familiar. He liked that. He hoped it didn't wind up biting him in the ass, but he liked it.

The elevator didn't take long to deliver them to Rec's floor. The carpet along the floor didn't impede the running of his chair's wheels at all.

He loved the way it smelled in Rec's apartment—totally rich and spicy and Rec all the way.

"You need a glass of water or anything before we get distracted by the sex sling set up in my bedroom?" Rec asked him.

"No. No, I'm okay…. There's really a sex sling?"

"There is really a sex sling. I'm going to put you in it and fuck you until you scream for me." Rec sounded absolutely serious.

"I… is it safe?" What if he fell? Could he fall?

"Absolutely safe. You'll be strapped in. The leather will smell amazing. Especially when it mingles with the scent of sex."

He didn't know, but he was going to try it. He never backed away from a new sensation.

"I love that look of determination you get once you've set your mind on something." Rec helped him stand and supported him along the hall to the bedroom.

"Do you? Do I?" Really?

"Yeah. It's pretty cool. It's how I know you're going to get better and get back to work."

"I am. I only have so many talents."

"Don't sell yourself short." Rec pointed to a contraption hanging from the ceiling. "Ta-da!"

"Wow…." That was…. Wow.

"I know it looks intimidating, but it's pretty easy. You'll see. All you have to do is trust me."

"I do." How would this work? Seriously?

"You're going to have to stand for a moment on your own. You think you're up to that?"

"You'll be right here? In case?"

"I'm not going anywhere. I need to get you into the sling after all."

"Okay." He nodded and trusted—standing on shaky legs.

"I'm going to strip you first. I'll be quick." Rec suited actions to words, quickly divesting him of his clothing.

He panted, Rec like a whirlwind around him.

Once he was naked, Rec began tilting him backward. "Stay stiff. I'll make sure the sling catches you."

He tried not to panic, but he did. This was scary.

"Easy. I've got you, and I won't let you fall, even if the sling does." As Rec spoke, Barclay felt the touch of leather against his back.

"I—I—okay…." Breathe. Breathe. "I can't fall again."

"Nobody is falling." Rec stroked his spine, and then Barclay felt the leather against him again, it and Rec supporting him as he became horizontal. "Believe in me, baby. I will never let you down."

Tears leaped to his eyes, but he was caught, was breathing.

"There, see? You're not going to fall." Rec wrapped straps around his arms and his legs, binding him in the sling.

"This is weird." But he was okay.

"Does it feel like you're floating?" Rec asked, fingers sliding on his skin.

"Uh-huh. A little. I'm okay?"

"You're totally fine. Look." Rec grabbed the chains that hung from the ceiling and tugged on them. "It's not going anywhere. All you have to do is lie back and enjoy it. Anything starts to hurt, you let me know and we'll adjust stuff."

"This is…. I've never thought…. Wow."

"I hope that's a good wow," Rec murmured, letting go of the chains and moving to stroke Barclay's skin.

"An overwhelmed wow. This is very new." He was beginning to relax, though, and remember how to breathe.

"It'll be very good," Rec promised, moving him slowly in the swing, hands remaining on him. "Rest your head back, baby. Relax. Breathe."

Right. Breathe.

"You can take as long as you need to acclimatize. I'm just going to touch you." Rec plucked gently at his nipples.

It was strange to be up here, relaxed, comfortable.

Rec began to drop kisses on his face, lips open and warm, hot. He moaned softly, tongue sliding against his own lips as he chased those kisses. They continued to elude him, Rec's kisses dancing merrily on his skin.

"There you go. You're here with me now."

"Yes." He was. He was here.

"Good." Rec's lips finally landed on his and stayed, the kiss soft and steady, long. Suddenly he was floating, relaxed, and he melted in the straps.

The kiss went on and on, Rec's tongue sliding into his mouth to tangle with his own. He felt that touch all the way to his balls, his body tightening.

Rec's fingers were warm, almost soft against his sac, holding him gently. Rec rubbed his thumb against the base of Barclay's cock, back and forth.

His breath sped, his heart rate zooming.

Rec ended the kiss, lips sliding along his face. Soft kisses landed next to his cheek, and he turned to join their mouths. Rec smiled as their mouths met again, the kiss lopsided, and the sling swung, moving him in the air.

He gasped, but he didn't fall. He was well held. The swing kept moving, the feeling of floating increasing with it. He could feel the air touching him.

Then Rec began to touch him as well, stroking his ass, his belly, his shoulder.

"Are you flying, B?"

"I think so. This is… it's so new."

"Yeah. You should enjoy the newness of it while it's still new. And I'm right here—I'm not going anywhere."

He closed his eyes, trying to comprehend this, understand what he was experiencing.

"Is everything comfortable? There's no reason for you to be hurting at all in this thing."

"Yes. This is… it's easy. It feels good."

"Excellent. That was the idea. I figured it would be ideal. Can you smell the leather? Is it sexy?"

He took a deep breath, focused. "I can! I hadn't noticed before."

Rec grinned, fingers dancing over his skin. "It's a feast for all your senses—not just touch."

"I can't touch. I can only feel."

"Well, feeling is the same sense as touch. I like that you keep me on my toes."

Who had said that to him? Ever.

Rec began to kiss him, leaving little busses all over his body, beginning with his shoulders. His nipples drew up, a dull ache starting.

"Mmm… these are calling to me." Rec dropped a really short kiss on his right nipple, then blew on the left.

"Are they?" Oh, that felt good.

"They really are." Rec flipped his tongue back and forth across each hard bit of flesh.

Barclay moaned as electricity shot through him.

"Loudly. Begging me to do this." Rec licked both nipples. "And this." Rec sucked each one for a scant moment.

Barclay gritted his teeth and wanted to scream.

"I like to hear what you're feeling," Rec told him.

"What does that mean?" He didn't understand.

"You're grinding your teeth, and that makes me think you're holding back a moan or something. You don't have to do that—in fact, I don't want you to. I want to hear every sound my touches and kisses and making love to you brings out of you. No matter what it is."

"I don't want to embarrass myself."

"You think your sounds are going to be embarrassing? Did someone say something to you at some point? Because me? I love sex noises. I mean love them. They turn me on. They tell me I'm on the right track or that I'm not. They're all good to me." Even as he spoke, Rec continued to touch him, to make him shiver with pleasure.

"They do?" He got that. Rec's words turned him on in the best way.

"Absolutely." Rec kissed his belly button, licked his tongue through it.

A laugh exploded out of him, surprising the hell out of him. Rec laughed with him.

"God, I love that sound. I really do."

"That tickled." And it made him shudder.

"How about this?" Rec leaned back in and, right next to his navel, pressed his lips hard and blew, making a long, loud noise.

He tried to curl in, but he couldn't. It wouldn't work. Rec laughed and blew again. Then the touches turned to long licks, Rec sucking along his skin.

"Oh. Oh that…. Thank you."

As a reply, Rec hummed, the sound sending vibrations running up along Barclay's skin, making it tingle. The wet lines left behind turned cold, leaving him shivering.

He shivered for a different reason when Rec bit at his hip, mouth hot, teeth sharp. "Please!" The word tore from him.

"Please what?" Rec asked, rubbing his cheek along Barclay's cock.

"Can you do that again?"

"I most certainly can." Rec bit at his hip again, then dragged his teeth along Barclay's skin.

He curled his toes, his fingers becoming fists.

"You going to vocalize how it makes you feel?" Rec bit his other hip.

"I—" He didn't know.

"Just don't hold back, okay?" Rec bit one more time, then did that teeth-scraping thing again, making his whole body tingle.

A bite to his nipple made him cry out; the hand nudging his balls made him grunt. Rec touched him all over, but none of the touches were the same: pinches and bites, licks, strokes. One thing that did stay the same—he had Rec's entire focus.

He twisted in the straps, unable to get away.

"Your belly is beautiful when you move like that." Rec pressed his hand against Barclay's stomach. "Such a strong core."

Heat flooded him, and he sort of wanted to cry with the praise.

Rec kissed his belly, sucking and licking. Was he going to leave bruises?

He didn't care. Rec could do anything, everything, to him.

Like Rec had heard him, the suction increased, pulling at his skin. He felt each tug in his balls.

He let himself cry out, once, twice, over and over. Rec moaned whenever he did and worked harder to get him to make more noises. Finally he stopped worrying and simply *felt*, letting himself go.

Rec seemed to know, and his explorations slowed, became more deliberate.

He swung back and forth, swaying nice and slowly as he waited for Rec to do the next thing.

Rec mouthed his wrist, warm lips tickling, making him squirm as best he could.

"That tingles all the way up."

"That's a good thing." Rec nibbled some more, then began to kiss his way up to the inside of his elbow.

"Uh-huh…." It was. It was a magical thing.

Rec lingered on the sensitive flesh there, licking and nuzzling against it. The barest hint of whiskers brushed him as Rec rubbed a cheek along the inside of his arm.

"This is… it's something else."

He felt Rec's smile against his skin. "I knew you'd enjoy it."

He'd never had a lover who was so thoughtful. Hell, he hadn't had a lot of lovers, just a lot of fuck buddies.

Rec stepped away a moment but was back before he could even form any sort of protest to throw a light blanket over Barclay's torso. Then Rec kissed his right ankle, lips soft but not so soft that it tickled.

He didn't know what to think. He didn't know what Rec was planning.

It turned out it was more of the same—slow, warm kisses and firmer nibbles from his ankles all the way up past his knees. Rec's lips sent tingles along his legs and hips that continued into his balls.

He began to shake as his muscles fought the need to relax, to give in. Rec stroked his legs in long sweeps from bottom to top.

"Easy now—trust the sling. It'll support you."

"I'm trying. I am. I'm sorry." He couldn't stop.

"You don't have to keep apologizing." Rec ran his hands along the inside of Barclay's legs again, then spread them wider and kissed his inner thigh, right up near where it met the rest of his body.

He whimpered softly, his eyes crossing.

Rec made him crazy using lips and tongue and teeth. There were places he was sure Rec was drawing up marks and others where the touches were so light he couldn't be sure he'd actually felt them.

It was wonderful and crazy-making all at once.

Rec's cheek nudged his balls, the touch gentle but startling, and he struggled to spread.

"You don't have to do anything but lie there, B. I've got this." Rec stood and spread his legs, then adjusted something on the straps of the sling, and suddenly his legs were being supported at that width.

He gasped, the motion a little wild, a lot wonderful. "Whoa."

Rec stood again and smiled down at him. "And look—you're now at the perfect height for me to fuck you." Rec moved the swing, sending him away, then bringing him back in again over and over.

He tensed, making sure it would hold, but it looked like it was going to.

"It's safe—you're good." Rec slid his hands to Barclay's ass, cupping his naked flesh. Both thumbs rubbed his crack and pressed against his hole like a promise.

His eyelids went heavy; his lips parted.

Rec's fingers disappeared for a moment, then came back to slide along his hole, slick with lube. God, it felt good, necessary.

"Sweet hungry hole," Rec moaned. Rec kept saying things that made him feel so good, like he was sexy, special.

Rec fingerfucked him, gliding easily in and out, Barclay's body gripping Rec's finger, encouraging it to stay in.

"Gotta get you open for me. Spread you wide so you can take my cock. You fit perfectly around me. Can you feel it?"

He whimpered, nodded. "I can. I... I feel spread wide."

"You are." Rec crooked his finger inside Barclay and hit that special spot. His whole body lit up, and he moaned, his hole clenching.

Rec pushed a second finger in with the first, stretching him wider. It was going to take Rec all day to get him open at this rate.

Somehow he didn't think Rec would be too worried, too disappointed about that fact.

Rec spread both fingers wide, then shoved them deep, hitting his gland and making his whole body sing. "Mmm... there you are."

Barclay tried to lift his head and focus.

"Just relax, B. I've got this. I've got you." Rec hit his gland a few more times.

"Oh Jesus! Fuck!"

"Soon as you're good and open. I'm not going to leave you hanging, you know that." Rec pushed in a third finger, and it was a good stretch, opening him. The burn was perfect. "From here I can fuck you, press my thumbs in alongside and stretch you wide."

"Oh God." He'd never asked for that before, never thought to want it, but now suddenly, he did. He really did.

"Do you like that, hmm? The idea of me spreading you wide."

How was he supposed to answer that? And why did Rec saying things like that turn him on so much?

"You don't need to be ashamed of it, B. I want to revel in it. In you."

"I want to. I mean, I want to know."

"I want to share everything with you. Everything I know." Rec pulled his fingers out, then slicked them back up and pressed four into him.

"Oh." His belly drew up, going tight and hard.

"Just keep breathing. You can take this."

"Yes." He wanted to. Needed to, maybe.

Rec pushed his fingers in slowly, opening him wider than he thought he'd ever been. The burn was perfect, though. A soft, deep sound pushed out of him, drawn from him.

"So hot and tight. You're perfect inside. Burning silk."

"It aches. So good." He could feel every finger.

"It's just going to get better." Rec kept pushing his fingers in deeper; then he turned them.

Barclay gasped, his toes curling. His legs drew up, or tried to.

"Don't worry—there's enough room for my fingers. I promise."

"I believe you. I do." Oh fuck. That felt so good.

Each movement from Rec was huge, echoing through his entire body. He shuddered, his bones feeling like they were going to shake apart.

Rec placed random kisses over his body as that hand moved inside him. Belly, nipples, neck, face. As if Rec was adoring him. He couldn't breathe, but he could.

When Rec pressed their mouths together, his lungs filled with air. He gasped, his whole world tightening to Rec—even his air was Rec's.

Everything about this was different, was new, and he didn't want it to end, even though he thought he might expire at any moment from pleasure overload.

"You're okay, baby. This is a good space. You're safe here."

Rec's words calmed him somehow, eased him, even as the pleasure pushed him higher.

He finally leaned into the straps and gave in, body and soul.

Rec seemed to know when he did it, a pleased hum sounding, the fingers inside Barclay moving faster. His body accepted, took, wanting more.

"You're ready for it to be me," Rec noted. "You want me to fuck you, to stretch you wider than that with my thumbs at the same time."

"Yes. Yes, please." He was more than ready.

Rec's fingers circled inside him a few more times before coming out. He'd never noticed how empty he was before, without someone inside him.

Rec took his time, putting a condom on his cock and slicking it up, Rec dragging his fingers along his own flesh. Barclay watched, licking his lips as he imagined that cock sliding into him, filling him up.

"You ready, B?"

"I am. More than." He tried to spread wide.

Rec grabbed his hips and pressed his cock against Barclay's hole. Then, very slowly, Rec pulled him close, the thick heat spreading him open millimeter by millimeter. He closed his eyes, focusing on the stretch, the pleasure.

Time seemed to stop; all that existed was him and Rec, their bodies moving together. Rec had his fingers wrapped around Barclay's hips, pulling him into each thrust.

Christ. Christ, his belly tightened up, and his eyes rolled back into his head.

"Stunning. Beautiful. My lover. My boy." Rec thrust as he spoke, rocking Barclay.

He couldn't answer, only nod and gasp and feel.

"You going to come for me, B? Gonna spread your jism up your belly? Gonna squeeze me tight?" Then Rec pressed his thumbs in alongside his cock.

The stretch was fucking amazing, wider than the four fingers earlier. Wider than he'd ever been stretched.

"Please," he whimpered. "Please, I need you."

"Right here." Rec slammed in, hitting his gland, those thumbs still keeping him open.

He cried out, pleasure tearing through him.

"Hold on, don't come yet. I want you to wait as long as you can."

He nodded, the request seeming so difficult but so reasonable. At least it was reasonable until Rec found his gland with every thrust, making the pleasure huge.

"I—" Oh damn. Christ.

Rec ran his thumbs up and down along his stretched hole until every nerve was firing off. Another hit to his gland and it was like an explosion was going off inside him, then another and another.

"Okay, B. Let's go together. I want you to come on my cock and make me shoot."

"Jesus." He cried out, the words making him dizzy.

"Not Jesus. Sex. Coming. Now!" Rec shouted, slamming into him several times in a row, his gland taking a beating that his balls couldn't resist.

He shot, his world going sparkly around the edges. Rec cried out, jerking into him a few more times before he froze and shuddered, cock throbbing inside Barclay.

Rec rested, using the sling to keep himself up, one hand resting on Barclay's belly.

He didn't know what to say. That had been amazing.

"You want to swing for a while?" Rec asked. "Just lie here and float?"

"Yeah. It's... easy."

"I'm glad." Rec kissed him softly before pulling out. "Damn. You feel so good, I didn't want to come out."

"I'm empty now," he whispered.

"I could help you with that," Rec offered. "I have a plug I could put in you. The perfect comfort."

"That's not weird?" To want it?

"I don't think it's weird at all, B. I think it's wonderful that you can recognize your needs—and share them with me."

He met Rec's eyes, worried, but the look on Rec's face was warm, happy, not mocking.

"What'll it hurt to give it a try? You've already discovered something new and awesome today."

"It won't. It won't hurt."

"No. I'm going to use a smallish one. Just so you feel it—but it won't stretch you very much, and it totally won't hurt. Plugs usually don't."

"I want to try." His cheeks were going to catch on fire.

"I think you're going to love it." Rec stroked his face. "You don't need to be embarrassed. Not for a second. What gets you off, what makes you feel good   it's all good."

"I guess. This is all... real new."

"I know. You're enjoying it, though, aren't you? Getting a lot out of it...?" Rec wasn't telling him. He could see that Rec genuinely wanted to know his thoughts.

"I just.... It's big. This whole thing is big, but I want it." He couldn't quite meet Rec's eyes.

"I want it for you. I want it with you." Rec kissed him. "I'm just moving to the chest in my closet. I'm not leaving the room."

"Okay. I believe you." Rec liked him. Rec was good to him so far.

Rec continued to talk to him, babbling about the plug. "I've got a nice plug here. Not as small as some, but not by any means large. I think it's just right if you'll pardon the three bears reference. Bears. Oh, that's funny."

He blinked; then he started to chuckle, his laughter joining with Rec's.

Then suddenly Rec was next to him again, solid and smiling and right there. Rec put the plug on his belly, the cool metal quickly warming.

It was surprisingly heavy, solid. Smooth.

"I'm going to slick it up and slide it into you, and then you can float here for a while. I'll stay with you." Rec's hand was hot on his skin.

"It's not... selfish?"

Rec blinked at him for a moment, clearly surprised. "No, it's not. Why do you think it might be?"

He shrugged, not sure what to say.

"You're not being selfish, okay?" Rec kissed the tip of his nose, making him smile, then moved between his legs again.

One finger slipped into his hole, the cool lube feeling nice, even if it warmed up quickly. "You are empty, aren't you? This will feel so good."

Barclay trusted Rec, believed what he said. He took a deep breath, moaning in disappointment as Rec's finger disappeared.

"Easy, easy. I'm going to put the plug in now."

"I like your touch."

"Then you should have it a little more, eh?" Two fingers pushed into him this time, Rec spreading them wide and sliding them in and out. Rec rubbed Barclay's belly with his other hand.

"Oh...." Could he want this? Again?

Rec's touch warmed him slowly, warmed him deeply. He moaned, his eyes crossing with his pleasure.

"Yeah, that's it. All you have to do is relax and enjoy this. That's the whole point, B. Find a place to float, to be inside pleasure."

"You're so good to me. Seriously."

"You deserve someone who is." Rec made the contraption swing gently, adding to the sensations.

"Oh God." It felt so good.

Rec didn't seem to be in a hurry to stop, either. The touches continued along with the gentle rocking of the sling.

"Tight, sweet little hole," Rec whispered.

He arched, the words making him want to preen.

"Mmm. You want so well. You're starved for attention, for sensation."

He hadn't thought so, but every touch Rec gave him soaked into him and left him wanting more.

"I'm going to put in the plug now, leave you tingling and warm from my fingers."

"Okay. God, I feel good."

Rec beamed. "I'm so glad. So glad."

Rec's fingers disappeared again, but this time, the hard metal of the plug pressed against his hole, sitting there like a promise.

"What do I do?"

"Just lie there, B. I'll get this in there, but I'm going to take my time. You should enjoy the insertion as much as the prep. Then you'll be filled for as long as you need." Rec pushed the tip of the thing into him, then turned it, the sensations big. Rec grabbed a chair and sat, eye level to his hole. "I want to watch you take it."

He whimpered. He actually whimpered. Rec's words were like magic, and they made him feel sexy, hot. Wanted.

"Sweet, swollen little hole." Rec blew a stream of air against his body.

It made him shiver and moan.

"Mmm. Yeah, beautiful boy."

The words soothed his soul deep down.

Rec continued to play with the plug, pushing it partway in and twisting it, tugging it out, pushing it in and out about an inch in quick succession. Then he pushed it in several inches, slow and easy. "I can see you stretch, see you taking it in."

"I can feel it."

"Does it feel good?" Rec turned the plug inside him again.

"Yeah. Yeah, it feels… hot."

"Good." Rec kept playing with him, sliding and turning the plug, the sensations growing upon each other. "Just a little bit longer."

"Okay. I'm okay. Really." More than.

"You're good in fact." Rec kissed the tip of his cock, then settled the plug in. Just like that, it was sitting there inside him.

"G-good. Fuck." His belly went tight.

"Good deal." Rec stayed where he was and rested a cheek against Barclay's inner thigh. The warmth was perfect.

He closed his eyes, breathing, floating. He'd never experienced anything like it. There was pleasure, warmth, comfort, happiness. All thanks to Rec.

Chapter Six

REC BROUGHT the just-delivered steak dinners into the living room where Barclay was dozing on the couch, looking at ease and relaxed. He'd known that the sling would go over well. And the plug proved that while Barclay might not know anything about the lifestyle, he was a born sub and not afraid to explore the things his body ached for.

"Hey, B. Supper is here." He spoke quietly so he didn't jerk Barclay awake, but really, it was time for food and companionship.

"Oh God. I'm sorry. I was just zoned out." Barclay tried to sit up, to figure out what to do.

"Don't worry about it—that's kind of what I was going for, so it's all good." He set the food on the coffee table. "I got UberEATS to bring us steaks from the Keg. I know it's expensive, but I wanted to indulge you."

"You're too nice to me. I can pay my half."

"You can get the next one," he suggested. They didn't need to worry about exact sharings or anything like that.

He got them both set up and then sat next to Barclay, enjoying the heat from his lover's body. Barclay kept kissing, kept reaching for him. Kept stroking his belly, his legs.

"Aren't you hungry?" Not that he was complaining about being loved on.

"Yes. Sorry. You're addictive a little." Barclay turned a sweet pink.

"You don't have to apologize for wanting to kiss and touch me. I like it when you do. I just don't want you passing out from hunger either."

"And the steak smells like heaven on earth."

"Yeah, it does." He set Barclay's container on his lap and offered over some utensils. "Let me know if you need anything."

"I'm not high maintenance."

Sean Michael

"Who called you high maintenance?" Had one of Barclay's past lovers said that?

Barclay hummed, sidestepping the question, and took a bite of steak. Rec shook his head. Barclay needed to open up to him. To trust him.

He grabbed up his own plate, though, and turned his attention to his food. Which was very good indeed.

Barclay ate eagerly, then reached for his crutches, carefully moving into the bathroom. Rec thought he was moving easier now. He liked to think the relaxing afternoon had something to do with that.

He needed to do some deep tissue massage, push Barclay into a deeper relaxation. That would go along nicely with some conversation once Barclay got out of the bathroom.

Barclay came out, face washed, grinning at him. That's what he liked to see. He smiled right back.

"Hey." Barclay crutched to him, eased himself down.

Reaching out, he settled his hand on Barclay's thigh. He loved touching this man. The muscles jumped for a second, then eased under his touch.

"How does a massage sound, B? Like the perfect accent to a great day?"

"Are you sure? I sort of owe you one."

"I'm not the one in recovery," he noted. He didn't need a quid pro quo. "Come on. Let's get you laid out on the couch."

"If you're sure...." Barclay came right to him.

"I'm totally sure. I wouldn't have offered if I didn't want to." He helped Barclay get laid out, then straddled the lovely ass and began digging in. He hated how worried Barclay was about being cared for. "So, what do you think about the sling?"

"It was amazing. So relaxing. Seriously."

"And you like the plug too, eh?"

Barclay flushed, the color climbing up his spine. "Yeah."

"You don't have to be embarrassed." Rec began to rub Barclay's shoulders. "That's what BDSM is about, you know? Exploring new things. Finding out what works for you. Really digging into it."

"I never.... I don't know anything about it."

"But you know you enjoy the sling and a plug. I bet you'd like to explore the plug thing more." He knew Barclay did. The man hadn't complained once about still wearing it.

B nodded, the sweet boy bright red.

"I'd love to do that with you. I have a few more plugs, but we could look them up online, see what intrigues you."

"How many are there? That's an industry?"

"Hell yeah it is. They come in all sorts of sizes, shapes, colors, and materials. There's even a site that does 'dragon penis' plugs."

"Dragon...."

"And demon, werewolf."

Barclay began to chuckle, the sound merry and making Rec want to laugh too.

"I swear to God I'm not making this up. The fantasy ones are actually quite beautiful. As are the glass ones. I don't know, though. I mean, they claim they're safe for use, but that would be a hell of a way to find out they aren't." He moved slowly down along Barclay's back.

"You.... I've never met anyone like you."

"Well, you know Tide and Lance and a few others from the gym, I bet. And we're all in the lifestyle. Or wasn't that what you meant?" He concentrated on the small of Barclay's back, thumbs working the little bundle of nerves.

"I meant you. You're...." B trailed off.

"I'm a Dom. So is Tide, but I'm guessing none of his vibes were headed your way." Chuckling, he moved down and began to massage B's gorgeous ass, rubbing both cheeks at the same time.

B arched and clenched around the plug. Needy. He approved. He rubbed it a little more, then put his thumb on the base of the plug and wiggled it around.

"Rec?" B arched, gasping softly.

"Feels good, eh?" He did it again.

"Uh. Uh-huh."

He kept doing it, stopping every few seconds to give Barclay a moment to catch his breath. "What else intrigues you? There's so much to explore."

"I don't know. I don't know what to choose."

"Hey, you can choose it all, you know? We have all the time in the world. I want to have fun with you. I want to show you stuff and explore everything you're even a little curious about."

"You say the best things."

"Yeah? I just want to make you happy, fulfilled." *Mine.*

"You don't have to work. I'm not... hard."

"It's making you feel good, though, isn't it?" He wasn't working toward an orgasm here—he was happy to keep Barclay floating and feeling nothing but good.

"Yes. God, yes. You're amazing."

He leaned forward to kiss the back of Barclay's neck. "So are you."

"Thank you."

Rec nudged the plug again, laughing as B arched. "Do you want more, baby? Something a little more challenging?" He moved down after that, working on the tops of B's thighs, then lower, then lower still to work on B's calves as he waited for an answer.

"I don't know how to answer that, Rec."

"Listen to your gut. Do you want to leave things as they are right now, or do you want a heavier plug, or a bigger one maybe?"

"I want more. God, why is that so hard to say?"

"Because many of us learn from early on that sex is shameful. That wanting it makes you a slut and that slut is a bad word. It's not. And there's nothing shameful about sex. That's one of the things the BDSM community embraces." He leaned down and bit Barclay's ass. "I think you're a delicious slut, B."

Barclay whimpered and arched, pushing up into the bite instead of away. Oh yes, that was exactly what Barclay was.

He bit again, then licked both bites, soothing the stings. "I'll give you more. I've got bigger plugs. I've got heavier ones. I have vibrating ones."

Barclay cried out, the sound muffled in his arms.

"I know you want to try it all, but we'll start with something heavier. That will let you stay in this lovely, melted state. We'll save vibrating for a day when the goal is to make you come." He dropped kisses along Barclay's spine, then rubbed the lovely skin. He would need to get up to grab a heavier plug, something to challenge B's hole, but not push too hard.

He left a last kiss on Barclay's ass, then got up. "I'll be right back. You can think of how a heavier plug is going to feel inside you."

"We don't have to...."

He snorted. "No, but we both want to, and that's all we need. Be right back." He knew exactly where the plug he wanted was, and he made short work of getting it.

Barclay was resting on his side, watching him, waiting for him. It sent a thrill of excitement through him. Barclay was his boy. Probably not ready to take that step yet, but that's what he was. It was there in every line of his body.

Everything about Barclay made him ache, made him need.

He returned to the couch and sat, offering Barclay the plug. This one was shaped more like a cock, but it had a heavy core.

"It's.... This one's sort of strong looking, huh?"

"Oh, I like that. It's the perfect description for it. Heft it a moment, feel the weight of it." He wanted Barclay to enjoy every aspect of this.

Barclay's eyes went wide as he lifted it. "It's heavy!"

"Indeed. Same size, more weight. You'll have to work a little harder to keep it in. Especially when you're walking. It's more intentional than the one currently inside you."

"Good thing I don't walk around much these days."

He chuckled. "You will walk some with it in, though. That's half the point of putting it in." It would be good practice in a safe space with something to focus on.

"You can roll onto your stomach again and I'll put a pillow under your hips. That'll put your ass up in the air for me." Look at that pretty blush. So hot. He reached out to touch one of those warm cheeks, stroke it. Then he grabbed a pillow. "I'm ready when you are."

Barclay rolled, the motion smooth. Easy. Hell yes. He'd read the man right.

He'd brought the lube out as well, so he was ready to make the exchange. Then he couldn't resist kissing Barclay's lovely ass again.

"Rec...." Needy boy.

He chuckled, fingers lingering on the lovely skin. "Yes?"

"You keep looking at my hole."

"Well... I have to if I'm going to change out your plug." That was just logic.

"Still... it's weird." And he'd bet Barclay thought it was hot too.

"You'll get used to it," he suggested.

"Oh."

He played with the plug, twisting it inside Barclay and moving it gently in and out. "Oh? Is that a good oh or a bad oh?"

"A turned-on oh."

That made him grin. "That's a very good oh." He would build on that. He tapped the tight little ring of muscles, then tugged it open again.

"Rec!"

"Need to take the plug out, B. Need to make sure you're stretched and open and slick when I push the heavier plug in." He'd noticed Barclay liked it when he talked about what he was going to do.

He loved how B blushed, how he heated.

Rec took his time with the plug removal. He enjoyed playing with it, making Barclay squirm and blush for him. In the end, he drew it out slowly, leaving his boy empty.

He tapped the empty, swollen hole, loving the way Barclay wiggled. Slicking up his fingers, he pushed two into Barclay, loving the heat that clamped down around him as soon as he did. He knew the cool lube would feel amazing. It was also warming quickly, so he added more to his fingers and fucked Barclay with them a few more times.

"Look at your pretty little hole, swollen for me, all pink."

"Shh... God...."

"No, I won't be quiet. You deserve to be praised, to know how sexy you are. How hot you make me." He curled his fingers as he drew them out, letting them stretch one side of Barclay's hole as he pulled slowly out. Then he patted Barclay's ass happily and grabbed the heavier plug.

He'd let B feel this one, make it good. To that end, he set it against Barclay's hole and pressed it there gently, watching as that little hole seemed to almost breathe around it—opening and closing.

He held it and waited. B would move eventually. He was right. After a minute or so, B wriggled, then arched back. Rec put pressure on, letting B's movements pull the tip of the plug in. He wiggled it, encouraging B to push back harder. Barclay groaned, slowly rocking back, taking it.

"That's it, B. Let your body pull it in. It knows what it wants. Don't fight it." He rubbed one asscheek with his free hand as he held the plug in place and watched B slowly draw it into himself. Fuck. It was amazing. "I could watch you fuck yourself for days, baby. Days."

"I'm not…."

"Shh. You are. But there's nothing wrong with that, remember? Sex is good. Needing it is good. If you've got someone to get off with, I guess. It's probably less good if you're on your own and only have your hand." God, he was babbling. He shut himself up by pressing the rest of the plug in. He circled it a few times, looking for the place where it seemed to rest the best.

"We've got someone to…."

Yeah, they totally did.

"Uh-huh. And I love getting off with you. I really do." He tapped the base of the plug, loving the way it made B jump. Then he kissed both asscheeks. "We should get you up for a few minutes, so you can experience the heaviness of it with gravity."

"I…. Hand me my crutches?"

He held out his hands. "You can use me."

Barclay didn't hesitate for a second, which he appreciated, reaching out to take his hands. He gently tugged, letting B help himself more than anything. Once B was upright, Rec steadied him.

"Oh. Oh, I feel…." His eyes crossed.

Rec chuckled softly. "You can't stop there. You have to tell me how you feel."

"It's in me. Pushing at my hole."

"Yeah. You've got to work a little to make sure this one doesn't begin to drop out, hmm?" He kept hold of B's hands.

"Uh-huh." B's legs were shaky, the joints buckling at first, but he was getting it.

"You can do it." He started to walk backward, bringing B with him.

"I feel ridiculous, huh?"

"Really? Because you look sexy as hell. Having the plug in changes your gait."

"I used to be able to leap."

B was going to be walking on his own soon, and that had nothing to do with Rec. Barclay just needed to believe he could.

"You'll leap again." He gave B a wicked grin. "Maybe it would be more advisable to not do it when you've got a plug like that in."

"Yeah, that would be weird." B laughed for him, though, both of them moving around the room slowly.

"So, do you like the sensation?" He wanted B to like it. And he wanted B to admit it.

"It's weird. It makes me ache some."

"And it's making you hard." Rec pointed at B's cock, which was making a great comeback, pointing at him. It would be pointing at the ceiling soon enough.

"Yeah. Neat, huh?" Oh, that was a bright smile.

"Oh yeah, more than neat." He stopped walking, but encouraged B to walk right up to him. "We could have fun with that." He totally wanted to suck B off. No anal—this was B's time to enjoy the plug.

"Fun with what, Rec?"

"With your erection." He reached for it, wrapping his fingers around the hot length, which encouraged it to harden the rest of the way.

"Before I met you, I hadn't had an erection since I got hurt."

"What can I say? I'm inspiring. Actually, I think it's more that I was the first person who saw you as a sexual being and did something about it."

"You won't let me fall, right?"

"I will not let you fall. Not just now, either, hmm?" He stroked gently, slowly, working the long cock from base to tip.

Barclay moaned, rocking toward him. Rec kept working the lovely cock, squeezing tighter as he began to move his hand faster.

He could see the bliss in Barclay's face. He stole a kiss, wanting to taste that pleasure and joy for himself.

Barclay grabbed his shoulders, holding on tight, swaying in his hands. He wrapped his free arm around Barclay's waist, adding more support.

"How's that plug feeling?"

"Heavy. Good. I… I like the more."

"I'm glad." He rubbed their cheeks together, then turned it into a kiss.

Barclay dove into the kiss, leaning hard against him. Rec kissed him for a long moment, then pulled back long enough to murmur, "Trust in me and relax—I will not let you fall."

"It's hard to keep upright."

"You wanna do this on the couch, B? We could move there. Though I don't think it'll take very long before I make you come."

"You won't let me fall."

He appreciated the fact that this time it was not a question. "No, I'm going to make you come."

"Never come so much in my life."

"That's sad. I'm glad I'm fixing that situation."

"You are. It is. Please, don't stop."

"Not going to." He kissed B again, jacking harder. Standing like this meant they needed to do this quickly.

He slid his tongue through B's mouth, deepening the kiss as he used his thumb to play with B's slit. Barclay cried out into his lips, the lean body beginning to shake.

"I've got you," he whispered into B's ear. He wasn't about to let B down. Barclay was going to come. He was going to feel it happen with that plug pushing against his hole, filling his boy.

"Please. It's so big."

"Then come on. Come for me. Shoot while you're holding in that plug. It's going to make it different from anything you've felt before." He pressed his fingers tighter together around B's cockhead, thumb working the slit like it wanted in.

"Fuck. Fuck. Rec!" Barclay arched, the expression on the dear face one of pure hunger. Seed spread between them, wet and hot. Sweet.

The scent of Barclay's come hit his nose and Rec moaned. Fuck, he did love that smell. He ignored his own cock, which was hard and eager from touching Barclay, from smelling him. This was about Barclay right now.

He continued to hold on, rubbing their cheeks together as he let B drift back down to earth.

"I want...," Barclay moaned.

He rubbed their lips across each other. "What do you want, B?" He was willing to give Barclay pretty much anything.

"Your cock. I want to suck you."

"Like I'm going to say no to that." He took a hot kiss, then drew Barclay back to the couch—it would be easier on his boy if he could sit.

Besides, they both liked it when he fucked Barclay's mouth, when he controlled it.

He hurried a bit. He could all but feel that hot mouth around his cock and he wanted it now.

Rec helped Barclay sit, easing him down. Then he climbed up, pushing up tall, and Barclay moaned for him, sweet and soft. The moan opened Barclay's mouth for him, and he slid his cockhead along the plump lips, groaning at the delicious sensation.

Fuck, he wanted this.

Barclay slid his tongue along the tip of his cock, dragging it along the slit. A shudder moved through Rec.

"Fuck!" Rec tried to catch his breath as he wrapped his fingers around Barclay's head. He wasn't going to take over and fuck that sweet mouth. Not yet. Not. Yet.

First he was going to let B ramp him up.

"Your mouth is like magic," he told Barclay, hoping to encourage more exploration. Just more.

Moaning, Barclay wrapped his lips around the tip and began to suck.

"Oh yes." He closed his eyes for a moment, just concentrating on the feeling of Barclay's tight lips, of the heat of his mouth and the slap of his tongue. Then he made himself open his eyes so he could watch Barclay's face and see those swollen lips holding tight around his cock.

B's eyes were closed, the expression one of pure bliss. Just this amazing peace. God, yes.

Between the sling, the plug, coming, and now this, Barclay was proving to be a true sub, happiest when he was fulfilled and could take comfort and joy from giving a blow job. That made them both very lucky men.

Him, most of all. For so long now he'd been looking for someone to care for.

He groaned as Barclay's suction got stronger, B's head beginning to bob now, taking more of him in. He watched as his cock became slick, shiny from B's mouth. He curled his fingers into B's scalp as he tried to keep still.

He wanted to fuck Barclay's face, but he needed to wait. Just a little longer. The anticipation was building nicely.

He swallowed a few times, his eyes glued to Barclay's face, to the pleasure he read there. God, Barclay was beautiful—even more so like this.

Barclay slowly stroked his thighs, petting him, encouraging him. He took that as a sign and began to rock, sliding his cock deeper with every stroke. He could feel the pleasure building with each push, with every suck. Barclay took him and took him.

"Oh fuck, your mouth is so hot. You're fucking amazing." He moved faster, hips rocking in short, sharp jabs that slid his cock along Barclay's tongue and deep into his throat. "I could do this every day forever."

Barclay swallowed hard.

"Fuck!" That was going to make forever very hard—he was coming down Barclay's throat the next time that happened.

Barclay groaned and swallowed hard, eyes flying open to watch him.

He thrust shallowly several more times, then thrust deep, crying out Barclay's name as he came. His balls emptied down Barclay's throat, his own body bowing.

Barclay took every inch, every drop.

He was amazing, and Rec knew he was falling for the guy. Hard.

"Sweet boy. Fucking gorgeous mouth."

Barclay pinked, but he also looked very pleased at the words.

Rec tugged his cock out of Barclay's mouth, wiped a spot of spunk from the corner of Barclay's lips, then pushed it in for Barclay to suck clean. He moaned as Barclay's lips closed around his finger, the suction as eager as it had been around his cock.

Fuck, that was special.

He sat next to Barclay, fingerfucking the swollen lips. Finally, he groaned and tugged his finger out. "You're something else, B."

"This is…. Thank you."

"You're welcome. And thank you." He leaned his head on Barclay's shoulder. Barclay reached up, hands warm on him.

"Mmm. I don't want you to go." Oh, that was a good idea. "You should move in."

"Yeah, yeah. I'd love to spend the night, if you don't mind. Love to."

"Not just for the night. You should *move in* move in. There's the elevator, the actual furniture, hot-and-cold-running sex…."

"But you don't know me. What if I'm… bad."

"Seriously? I've had you sleep over for the weekend and now you're back. Hell, you let me put you in a sling and fuck you blind. If either of us is bad, it's me." He took Barclay's hand. "Look, we can keep it casual. It'll just make it easier for you if you're here. Quick to the gym, easy to get around… daily massages."

"Will it be easier for you, though?"

"I want to spend time with you, and with you living here, I get more of that." He honestly wanted to have Barclay here. With him. "Say yes."

"Maybe we try it for a couple days? See what we see?"

"Sure." He gave Barclay a quick kiss. "Good. I didn't want to have to see you go off tonight."

"No. No, I want to stay."

"Then you'll stay. Open-ended."

"We'll have to talk about money for rent, huh?"

"I own the place outright, so I don't really need rent. Your share of utilities and groceries works, though."

Barclay rested hard against him. "I can't believe this is happening."

"I'm glad it is. I love having you here, being with you. It hardly makes sense to have you go all the way up to your place every day just to come back down for the gym or to spend time here." He was happy about this. And he couldn't wait to show Barclay all the different ways they could play. Hell, he couldn't wait to see how much they could push with the plugs.

Barclay petted him, stroking his belly, loving on him.

"And just in case you think I'm being selfless or something— I'm doing this for me as much as you."

"Are you? You want this?" Barclay melted into him.

"I do." He wrapped his arm around Barclay, keeping him close. "I really like you. I like being with you. I like making love to you."

"Yeah. I—is it weird? To make this connection so fast? It seems weird."

"Do you believe in love at first sight?" Rec asked.

"I don't know. I don't *not* believe."

"Well, I was attracted to you from the start. And I wanted to go the extra mile for you. Every moment I stay with you, I care more about you. So… it may not be love at first sight, but no, I don't think it's weird how fast it's gone." Rec traced circles on Barclay's skin.

Barclay nodded, moaning for him, the sound so satisfied.

"I want to explore all the things that turn you on. Everything that makes you happy. I want to fulfill you." He didn't care if they called it love or BDSM or just fooling around. He needed to do it for Barclay.

"I want to be good for you."

"You are. You make me happy." He tilted his head, thinking about that. "It wasn't that I was unhappy before you. But you make everything bigger. Better. I'm happier now. It's deeper, somehow. If that makes sense."

"I think I'm figuring it out." Barclay hummed softly. "It's been a sad few months for me."

"I hope I'm making you happy." He thought he was blowing Barclay's mind with good things, but he didn't want to assume anything or put his thoughts down as Barclay's. He slid his finger along Barclay's cheek, looking into the blue eyes.

"You are. I didn't think I'd ever…." Barclay shook his head.

"Didn't think you'd ever what? Don't hold back." Rec wanted to know what Barclay was going to say.

"After the fall, it was bad."

"Physically or everything?" he asked. Barclay hadn't really talked much about the accident or his recovery, barring the basics Rec needed as the man's personal trainer. Oh man, did Barclay want someone new, given they were together now?

"I… I think…. It doesn't matter."

"Of course it matters. I want to hear your thoughts, B. You count, you know?" He hugged Barclay to him. "You do."

"I don't think it was an accident."

"That we met?"

Barclay shook his head.

"You mean you falling off the roof?" His eyes went wide. Wow. That was…. "Have you told the police?"

"No." Barclay pulled away a little.

"Okay. It's okay." He drew Barclay closer again. "It's okay. Can I ask why not?"

"They say I'm imagining it. That I'm just remembering the last person I saw."

"So you did talk to the cops when it first happened? I'm sorry they didn't believe you." He kept stroking gently, touching Barclay, keeping them connected.

"Yeah. I mean, maybe, but I don't think I'm lying."

"Well, what do you think happened? Who did this to you?" He was willing to form a posse and knock some heads together if needed.

"An ex. It was a thing. What if I'm wrong?"

"The same ex who pulled the ring right out of your nipple?" Rec was beginning to form a picture. And it wasn't a pretty one.

"It doesn't matter."

"Of course it matters—if you falling off the roof wasn't an accident, if you were pushed, then the person who did it should go to jail for attempted murder. I want him off the streets and safely away from you."

"It won't happen. I can't prove anything."

He sighed, holding Barclay close. "Are you sure? Surely you know if you got pushed or if you fell?"

"I saw him, watching me."

"That's creepy."

Barclay nodded, still refusing to meet his eyes. He took Barclay's chin in his fingers and tilted his head until Barclay was forced to look at him. "What?"

"I don't…. What if he wanted to kill me?"

"He pushed you off a roof—I don't think there's any 'if' about it." And that was scary. What if this guy wanted to finish the job. "Is he unhinged?"

"He thinks I'm worthless, more than anything. He didn't like being argued with."

"He sounds like a real asshole." Rec squeezed Barclay tight. "He sounds abusive as fuck. You know none of that is true, right? You're not worthless. You're special."

"I'm just a dude."

"'Just.' I don't know—I think you're pretty special." He really did. "Have you seen him since the accident?"

"Only once. He was there at the beginning, when I was drugged up."

"You'll tell me if you see him again, right?" He wanted to stay on the ball with this. He did not want Barclay having to face this alone.

"I won't. I don't want to see him."

"That sounds like a good plan."

Barclay chuckled softly, nodded. "Yeah. I think so."

He kissed the top of Barclay's head. "I've got you. I do."

"I don't want you hurt either, Rec."

"I won't be. I don't think that's an issue. I trust that you're here because you're interested in me and enjoying our explorations." He knew Barclay had a good heart.

"I am. I'm here because I like you. Because I like us."

"Then we're good." Tilting Barclay's head, Rec gave him a kiss, tongue sweeping through Barclay's mouth, tasting him yet again.

Barclay hummed and finally, blessedly, relaxed against him.

Good. Very good. He let his eyes close and enjoyed the moment.

Chapter Seven

BARCLAY WOKE up in Rec's bed, curled around Rec's pillow. Rec had gone to work, and he was… a slacker. A real slacker.

He made himself sit up and grab his phone, check Tumblr and Instagram, and then he got in his chair, butt naked, and started cleaning. It wasn't too bad—Rec obviously kept a fairly neat house. It felt good to be doing something, though. To be helping out.

He changed the sheets and ran the dishwasher, cleaned the bathroom, then took a shower.

He was back in the chair, still naked, when he heard the front door open. "Hey, honey, I'm home!"

"Hey you." He wheeled out, towel in his lap. "How was your morning?"

"Good. Look at you." Rec licked his lips and waggled his eyebrows. He was hot in a pair of Lycra workout shorts and a tight T-shirt.

"I just showered." And now he was tingling, all over.

"You look good enough to eat. Can I?" Rec came over and bent, taking a kiss.

"Are you…." He let himself kiss back, luxuriate for a long minute.

Rec drew back eventually and rubbed their noses together. "Am I what? Going to eat you? Absolutely yes! If it was something else, you'll have to let me know before I answer." Rec smile was warm, his eyes twinkling happily.

"I was going to ask if you were hungry."

"I'm hungry for you." Rec laughed softly. "God that was cheesy. True, though."

Barclay laughed and held on to Rec, letting Rec help him stand.

"Mmm. You smell good." Rec nuzzled his neck, then licked. "You really do. It's making me want to eat you up all the more."

"I can handle that. I know how. Give me all you have."

"Bed?" Rec suggested as he tugged off his T-shirt.

"I changed the sheets."

"Does that mean I need to shower too before I can use them?" Rec stripped his shorts off next, unapologetically naked.

"No. You smell good to me." It made him a little dizzy, honestly.

"Cool. I like how you smell all hot and sweaty too." Rec grabbed his hands and slowly walked him to the bedroom, leaving his chair behind.

He felt steadier every day, more sure. A part of that was Rec's belief that he could do things and the constant, solid support.

Rec grinned as they got to the bedroom and sat with Barclay on the bed. Before either of them said anything, Rec took another kiss, devouring his mouth. It felt so good, so right, and he couldn't bear to not touch, to not stroke Rec's needy prick.

Rec was ready for him, already heavy.

Groaning, Rec dropped his head back, exposing the long throat to him. He leaned in to kiss and lick the lovely skin, earning himself more noises from Rec. It felt good, to be able to adore, to love.

Rec wrapped an arm around him and fell back, bringing him down too. "You okay with your legs hanging off the bed like that?" Rec asked between kisses.

"For now." They were going to fall asleep, but for now they were fine.

"Say when they're not." Rec tugged on his lower lip, hands sliding up and down over his back.

"Uh-huh." God, he loved this. He let his own hands wander, sliding them on Rec's amazing skin. Rec's cock was hot, hard, pressing against his belly as he lay over Rec.

He moved experimentally, undulating carefully, and he managed to make the move without causing any pain. Rec's smile surprised him, pleased him, and Rec moved with him, rolling back against him. They found a rhythm, their bodies coming together in the best way.

"You're hungry, all right." He tweaked Rec's nipple, tugging a little bit hard.

Arching, Rec gasped for him, fingers digging into his skin for a second before Rec relaxed back onto the mattress. "Starving, B. You have no idea."

"No? You get excited with all those studs at the gym?"

"Nope." Rec drew his hands up along Barclay's sides, fingers firm on his skin. "I got excited thinking about you here waiting for me. It's exciting, having you live with me."

He arched under the touch, gasping softly as his muscles stretched.

"Let's move to the middle of the bed." Rec shifted, tugging him up along. Rec bucked slowly, smiling as Barclay moved on the big body. "That's better."

"It is. Thank you."

"It's always my pleasure to make sure you're in the best position you can be." Rec continued to touch him, fingers sliding along his skin, slowly, firmly.

"I'm going to get better and you won't have to."

"Are we going to do acrobatics once you're back in tiptop shape?" Rec asked, eyes dancing with amusement. "I might have to invest in a *Kama Sutra*."

"I might. You never know with me."

"I can't wait to find out!" Rec drew him down into another kiss, tongue opening his lips and pushing in. When the kiss was over, Rec leaned their foreheads together. "Did you have a good morning?"

"I cleaned up and took a shower, so yeah. I think I did okay."

"Good to hear. I'm glad you didn't start working out or anything. You need your day of rest in between to let your muscles heal. Once you're better, you can go back to full workouts every day, but for now…." Rec chuckled. "Sorry. We're in bed—I'm not your trainer right now, I'm your lover. Sorry." Rec nipped at the tip of his nose. "Wanna fuck?"

Barclay rolled his eyes, and then he started laughing, holding on to Rec as he went with it.

"Laughing at me." Rec pouted, but the look didn't make it to his eyes, which were laughing right along with Barclay.

"With you." He took a kiss, feeling free and daring. "And yes, I wanna fuck."

"You want to do the sling again, or you wanna lie on your belly, propped up on pillows?" Rec kept touching him, fingers sliding on his skin and leaving amazing tingles in their wake.

"This is good. We're here, right?" He didn't want to leave the bed. It was cozy and warm with Rec beneath him, and it smelled good, clean and like them. Like both of them.

He had a bed that smelled like him and his lover. How cool was that?

"Yeah, we're here and it's good." Rec nipped at his nose again, then rolled them, putting him beneath the strong body. Rec undulated against him, all their bits dragging in the most delicious way.

"Oh...." He tried to arch up, meet Rec, and he managed with just a few twinges.

"That okay?" Rec asked, rolling against him again. He swore he could feel the hairs on Rec's thighs against his balls.

"Uh-huh. It's okay. I'm okay."

"Okay." Rec chuckled again, then kissed him, stealing his breath on this one as their bodies worked to rub together.

Then he was so much more than "okay;" he felt almost normal.

Rec had the magical ability to move against him and touch him at the same time and make it all seem normal and natural and amazing too. "I'm going to turn you over, sweet boy, and take your ass. Make it last."

He moaned, the sudden image Rec put in his head intoxicating. Fuck yes, and also please.

He helped, but Rec did most of the work, putting him on his belly, then sliding a pillow beneath him so his ass was pushed up.

"Mmm... look at that. All mine."

He blushed, heat moving down his back.

Rec hummed, fingers sliding from his shoulders on down, taking the same route his blood had. "God, you make me ache. You and your sweet hole."

"Rec!"

"Hmm? Spread for me."

He did so automatically, Rec's word all he needed.

"Such a good boy. I'll keep you." Rec tapped his hole.

He jerked, pushing back without even thinking about it. More. He wanted more.

"Mmm... needy too. I approve."

He was, but because Rec seemed happy about it, he wasn't horribly embarrassed.

"More."

"Everything you can handle." Rec bit his asscheek playfully.

He yelped, but it was from surprise more than hurt, and Rec's chuckle made him smile. "Sorry. You surprised me."

"I'm always looking for new ways to give you sensation." Rec licked where he'd bitten and the sudden wet heat was enough to make him gasp.

"You're something else. A good lover."

"You're inspirational, B." Rec rubbed his cheek along Barclay's ass, then licked his crack from top to bottom, right across his hole.

He jerked away, the motion immediate, the heat huge. And Rec did it again, then again and again, his entire body lighting up from it.

"Please…. It's big."

"Just breathe and enjoy it." Rec didn't stop, the licking making Barclay shiver with how good it felt.

He wanted to touch himself, but more than that, he wanted not to, to let the pleasure go on and on and on. Rec certainly wasn't giving any indications that he was going to stop licking his hole.

His balls drew up, his thighs beginning to shake, and he needed more. Like Rec knew, he spread Barclay's cheeks and pushed his tongue right in.

"Oh God!" He cried out, shocked, unsure what to do.

Rec hummed and that made everything even bigger. Tongue-fucking him. That's what Rec was doing, pushing that tongue into him over and over.

He drove down into the pillow, trying to fuck himself, to get himself off. It wasn't enough, though, and Rec wasn't helping, not giving him any other sensation but that tongue pushing in and out of him. The pleasure was like nothing he'd ever felt before.

A coil of need tightened inside him, his entire body lighting up.

"When you're ready, I'm going to push inside you. Take you until you can't stand it another second and shoot your junk all over that pillow."

"Please. Please, I'm ready. I want you."

"You have to wait until I think you're ready." Rec continued licking.

"No fair. I need. God." He was going to lose his mind.

"I'm not going to leave you hanging."

He believed it. He did. He believed it, but he still begged.

And Rec still tongue-fucked him, sliding one hand down to stroke his balls.

He bucked up, the gentle touch seeming so huge.

It went on and on until he thought he was going to start screaming. Finally, Rec backed off and he heard the crinkle of the condom package opening and knew it wouldn't be long before he had Rec inside him.

He arched, feeling so loose, so easy. Two fingers moved in, slick and almost frictionless, and he arched back against them—he needed more.

Rec's fingers disappeared, and then he got what he needed, Rec's thick length nudging against him, slowly opening him up. He sighed softly, letting his eyes drop closed.

"You like that, B? Like feeling my cock inside you?" Rec kept pushing, sending his cock deep.

"Yes," he moaned, spreading wider so Rec could sink in farther.

"Yeah, I like being inside you too." Rec's voice had gone low and needy. He finally stopped moving forward when he was fully in, hips snugged up against Barclay's ass. Then he began to rock, staying buried.

Barclay whimpered and bucked back, trying to get more.

"Patience, B. We're going to take our time." Rec stayed right there, not speeding, not moving faster. Keeping complete control.

"Trying to be patient. Trying."

"Fact that you don't want to be means I'm doing my job." Rec pressed kisses across the back of his neck, adding sensations—making him want things to move along even more.

No matter what he did, Rec never sped up.

"Gonna make it last, B. Gonna make you beg for more." Rec's kisses moved lower, running from one shoulder blade to the other, tongue sliding on his skin.

"No fair…." God, it was hot, perfect.

"I'm going to make you come like you've never come before. I think that's plenty fair." Rec licked from the top of his spine on down, cock finally sliding partially out of him. Then the lick moved back up, Rec's cock pushing right back in. Barclay felt every centimeter, filling him up and making him ache.

More circling happened, making him shudder. He lost track of time, of everything but the cock inside him and Rec's body over him, so hot, so solid. So right there.

Time stopped, leaving him with low cries and a deep ache.

He nearly screamed when Rec began moving properly, thrusting into him and nudging his gland.

"Oh, you're ready for me now, aren't you?"

All he could do was nod.

"Yeah, I thought so." Rec moved faster, finding a good, solid rhythm that finally felt like it was building toward coming. Barclay met every single thrust, making his muscles work.

It felt good, being able to participate, to press back into each thrust. To make Rec moan the way he currently was.

"Don't stop, B. I want to feel you."

The words encouraged him, and he drove back onto Rec's cock.

"Fuck yeah." Rec thrust in harder, and coupled with his own movements, that slammed Rec's cock up against his gland in the best way. A low cry left him, and he repeated the motion, sending lightning through his body.

Rec moved with him so he wasn't doing all the work, but he found himself eager to be an active participant. The swing was amazing, but this meant he was getting better.

Sliding a hand beneath him, Rec squeezed his cockhead. "You're thinking too hard."

"Am I?" How did Rec know?

"Yeah. Just pay attention to your body—to the pleasure. Everything else is details and can be ignored until later." A soft kiss landed on his spine, sending little tingles out across his back. The second one joined up with the pleasure in his ass.

"Trying. I'm trying." God, he was hard and full.

"You're doing great. Gonna both come so hard. Hold on for it. Better if we last." Rec gasped out the words, clearly affected by what he was doing.

"Uh… uh-huh. Hold on." He could do that, hold on tight.

"Oh fuck. Yes. Oh God, that's good, B." Rec moved faster, wrapping the fingers of one hand around his hip and holding on. Rec kept touching his cock and balls with his other hand, the touches light, not enough to send him over, but definitely enough to add to the pleasure coursing through him.

"You can't... I can't hold on." He clenched his toes, squeezed them tight.

"S'okay. Me either." Groaning, Rec leaned his head against Barclay's back and wrapped his hand firmly around Barclay's cock. "Let's do it."

Yes!

They started moving with purpose, slamming together over and over, the pleasure overwhelming.

"You first! It'll make me." Rec squeezed his cock tighter, angle changing slightly so Rec's thrusts got his gland full-on each and every time.

That was an easy answer. Barclay took a deep breath, letting it out in a huff. Like that was a signal, his body let go, spunk shooting in several long pulses. The orgasm felt like it went on and on, each hit of Rec's cock against his gland sending another wave of pleasure through him like echoes.

Rec finally stopped thrusting, cock buried deep inside him as Rec panted against his back.

"Wow." He felt like he'd been put through a wringer. Not in a bad way, though. In this melted, sated, "I've had an amazing orgasm" way.

"Uh-huh." Rec was still panting. "Gimme a minute and I'll come out."

"Wish you could stay."

"Can't really with the condom." Rec laid his cheek flat on Barclay's back, nuzzling against him. "Or I would. That would be so awesome. Do it on our sides and just drift off all warm and snug inside your body...."

"Yeah." That sounded amazing. Perfect.

Especially when a moment later, Rec groaned and pulled out, leaving him so empty. Damn.

"We could get tested," Rec suggested as he got rid of the condom and grabbed some tissue, gently dabbing at Barclay's hole. "I've always used a condom, so I would be surprised if I was anything but negative."

"We could, but what if I'm not? Would you still want to... be with me?"

Rec turned him over gently, pulling away the pillow at the same time, which handily dealt with the wet spot. Then Rec began sliding the tissue on his belly, cleaning him. It wasn't until he was done that Rec rested next to him and looked him in the eye.

"Yes, I would. We'd have to keep using a condom, but it's not a deal breaker at all. It's better that we know if you are HIV positive anyway, so you can take preventative measures and keep testing." Rec kissed him softly. "Do you think you might be?"

"No. Not really. I always used a rubber, but… I don't know if I trust him."

"The guy who pushed you?"

He nodded.

Rec hugged him tight. "If you always used a rubber, you should be okay. But let's get tested even if we don't wind up going bareback. You need to know one way or the other. For your peace of mind."

"Yeah, I guess so. What can it hurt?" If he was positive, then he'd cope. He was good at coping, mostly.

"It's a little pinprick to take the blood. That's the only pain." Rec kissed him and tugged the covers up as he settled in close. "I know it's the middle of the day, but I'm feeling all lazy and melted and good. Wanna nap?"

"I do. Thank you for… everything." Mostly for the deep, stunning ache in the pit of his belly.

"Thank you, B. You make coming home a joy." Rec pressed another kiss to his cheek, eyes closing. "I'll make you something delicious for a late lunch after nappage."

"Mmm." He was fine. Just fine. "Sleep."

"Yes, Boss." Rec's gentle laughter followed him into his dreams.

Chapter Eight

REC HELD the door from the gym open for Barclay, then strolled with him toward the Swiss Chalet. He was feeling great. They'd had an amazing workout—Barclay really pushing today without feeling utterly spent at the end of their hour. It was a beautiful day. The results of their tests were supposed to come in today, and he was feeling very good about their prospects on that. And he and B were headed for what he had started thinking of as "their" restaurant.

He settled his hand on B's shoulder—his alternative to holding hands while both of B's were occupied.

Barclay was barely using the chair at the apartment, and they'd started discussing moving the few special things B had. He wanted his place to be home for B, and having his things there would make them both feel like his condo was exactly that.

His phone buzzed and he checked it eagerly, then shook his head. "Nope. Spam. We'll hear soon, though. They said today."

"It'll be okay, right?" Barclay looked back at him, grinned. "I mean, we're good."

He smiled right back. "We're good no matter what the results are, so yeah. It'll be just fine."

They got to the restaurant at the same time as someone else, and Rec stopped to let him go in first. He put his hand back on B's shoulder, narrowing his eyes as B's face went white.

"I...." Barclay rolled back, bumping into him. "I want to go."

"What's the matter, B?" He pulled Barclay a little farther out of the way so they wouldn't be even remotely in the path of the other guy at the door. The guy followed, though, and Rec's frown got stronger when he realized Barclay was staring at the man. "What the fuck?"

"I want pizza." Barclay was pale as a sheet. "It smells bad in here."

"Aren't you going to even say hi, baby?" the other guy asked, coming closer.

Rec didn't like the look of him and kept moving backward, pulling Barclay along with him. "Back off." He was going to get between them as it occurred to him that this was the ex.

"That's not very polite. You don't answer my emails; you don't answer the door. You're being a bit of a bitchy-poo."

Bitchy-poo? Really? This fucker was deranged.

"Rec, it's time to go."

"Yeah, I got that." He swung Barclay's chair around, nearly hitting another pedestrian. He gave them a curt nod and a quick "Sorry about that," before throwing a warning back at the asshole. "Either of us ever see your face again and we're calling the cops." Then he headed back to the gym. It not only was closer than home and safe, but that way this guy wouldn't see where they lived.

It occurred to him that it might be too late on that front—who knew how long this guy had been following Barclay, but at least this way there was a chance they were keeping their address under wraps.

It spoke to how upset Barclay was that he never so much as asked where they were going or complained about being pushed.

Tide was just coming out as they got there, and he held the door for them. "Forget something?"

"Yeah, something like that." He wasn't surprised when Tide followed them in; he felt like he'd worn that same frown himself when Barclay had first balked.

He pushed Barclay in toward the front desk so they couldn't be seen from the door, then crouched next to him as Tide stood close, arms crossed like the best bodyguard going in town. "Are you all right?"

"I...." B stared at him, shaking his head.

He put his hands on Barclay—one on his shoulder, the other on his leg. "It's okay. He can't get us in here."

"What's going on?" Tide asked quietly.

"Barclay's asshole ex is outside. He's the one who put B in the chair—pushed him off a rooftop—and now he's stalking B." It didn't matter if this was the first time the guy had approached Barclay since the hospital; it was clear from what he'd said that he was a stalker.

"Fuck that shit, I'm calling Union. He's a member who just happens to be a cop." Tide grabbed his phone and took a couple steps to the side.

"I want to go home. This is… this is fucked up." Barclay took a shaky breath. "You should stay here. I'll head to my apartment and he'll leave you alone."

"That's very noble of you, B." But it so wasn't happening. "However, I've got a better plan. We'll find out when this Union guy can come see us. If he can't come soon, we can always go home and wait there. I'm even willing to go to your apartment if you think that'll put him off our trail as far as where you really live goes. Hell, let's just go upstairs and spend an hour in one of the back rooms finding our centers before we have to go back out there again." Whatever they wound up doing, he was not leaving Barclay on his own. Not with that asshole in the wind. No fucking way.

"That's a good idea," Tide agreed. "Head upstairs and chill. Union will be a bit, and you two can get a juice, relax." Tide grinned at him, even though the expression didn't reach Tide's eyes.

"Yeah, that's a great idea. B needs something more substantial than just juice, though, after working out." He'd never checked the vending machines that closely. He supposed a protein bar would do for now.

"Go see if Jude's brought anything in today. He often does. I'm going to go stand at the door." This time Tide's expression couldn't be called anything but grim.

Rec took Barclay up to the elevator, refusing to even hesitate. Upstairs was safer.

He grabbed his phone as they went up and called the front desk. As luck would have it, Jude answered.

"Hi Jude. It's Rec, I'm upstairs with B. At the risk of being rude—would you happen to have anything we could munch on? Circumstances have us stuck here for a little bit, and B's just finished a tough workout."

"Of course! There is a lovely baguette upstairs and cheese and turkey, and there's a pasta salad and a fruit salad. Help yourself."

That sounded amazing. "Are you sure we're not taking your food?"

Jude laughed softly, the sound a touch self-deprecating. "I always bring in extras. Outside of my subspace, cooking is my happy place, and there's always more than we can eat."

"Well, thank you very much. It all sounds delicious."

"Enjoy!" Jude hung up.

Rec put his phone away and turned his attention to Barclay, who was just sitting there looking frozen. He crouched again so they could be at eye level. "Talk to me, B."

"I didn't expect to see him. I haven't seen a hint of him. Not since the hospital." Barclay looked right through him. "I never thought—how stupid of me, to think he'd never show up again." Barclay grabbed his hand, held on. "I probably overreacted, right?"

Rec didn't think Barclay had overreacted at all. It had been clear from his words that the ex was rather unhinged. And that he'd been watching Barclay, trying to keep in touch. "I think you did exactly the right thing. You didn't engage, and you got away as quickly as you could." He put his free hand on top of Barclay's and used both to squeeze. "I know you're probably scared, but we're going to deal with this right away. The cops aren't going to ignore you this time, I promise." And if this Union couldn't help, he'd go down to the precinct and find someone who could.

"I'm not scared. I don't think I'm scared. I'm... confused? I don't know what he wants from me. He doesn't like me."

Why on earth would someone not like his B?

"I think he likes you too much, and in a bad, obsessive way. I also think he's deranged, so trying to make sense of his behavior is only going to be an exercise in frustration." He squeezed Barclay's hand again. "Let's get something to eat—Jude has left some wonderful stuff in the fridge. I bet you feel more settled after we eat."

He found the food, making up delicious sandwiches and adding pasta and fruit. God, this was better than any restaurant.

"Look, babe. This looks amazing, doesn't it? Do you want water, B? Apple juice?"

"Water, I think. Thank you. God, I totally overreacted, didn't I?"

"No, absolutely not. That prick threw you off a roof." The more Rec thought about it, the more he believed it. Maybe Barclay couldn't remember it clearly, but that asshole had definitely meant Barclay harm. It had been written all over his crazy face.

"You believe me." It wasn't a question. Not at all.

"I do. I believed you anyway, but after seeing his face—" He shook his head. "—I don't have any doubt." He pushed Barclay's chair up to the table so he wouldn't have to transfer and sat next to him. "We're going to have to figure out an appropriate way to say thank you to Jude."

"Sure. I can pay to replace the food if you want? Or get flowers?" Barclay's hands were shaking violently, the water sloshing in its bottle. That calm facade was hiding a lot of fright.

"I'm pretty sure Jude would be insulted if we paid for the food. We'll figure something out." He took the bottle out of Barclay's hands and grabbed them with his own. Then he leaned their foreheads together. "I want you to close your eyes and breathe for me."

"Breathe?" Barclay sounded so confused.

"Yeah, just breathe with me. We're going to clear our heads a little, okay?" He closed his own eyes and took a deep breath in, nice and long and slow. Then he exhaled the same way before drawing in another breath.

His boy took a few minutes to get with him, to catch up, but soon they were breathing with just the fewest hiccups along the way. He chanced a quick peek, pleased that Barclay had his eyes closed too.

"Everything's going to be okay," he said quietly. "You're not alone. You don't have to deal with this by yourself."

"I've tried to be so cool," B whispered. "Brave and shit."

"Hey, until the other day I didn't even know you were pushed—that it wasn't an accident. I'd say you've been brave and shit for over a year now. It's time to share the burden and let me—and the community—help you, fight for you. We've got this. All together we've got this." He hugged Barclay tight. He'd come really close to missing out on this, to losing Barclay before he'd even found him.

"Together." The word sounded a little like a prayer in B's voice. "I'd like that, some help."

"You've got it. And not just me. Tide, Jude, Union. All the members here band together. You'll be safe, and that fucker doesn't know what's

about to hit him." He kissed B hard. "You think you can manage some of
this amazing food now?"

"Yeah. Yeah, I'm empty. Breakfast seems like a long time ago."

"Yeah, our granola was fine until that workout, huh?"

Barclay actually grinned for him.

He smiled right back and stole himself another kiss. Then he
sat back and grabbed his sandwich. He watched Barclay, though—he
wasn't going to eat until Barclay did.

Barclay lifted the sandwich and took a bite, chewing slowly,
and by the next bite, Rec thought color was coming back to Barclay's
face. He took a deep breath of his own, relaxing a little, then dug into
his own sandwich.

It was delicious, as was the pasta salad. And, as usual, they both
concentrated on eating rather than talking. Without consulting each
other, they both ate the fruit salad last. It pleased him that they were
so in tune in so many things.

"Maybe a fruit basket would make a good thank you."

"Sure. I'll order one. No problem." Barclay passed him the
pineapple. At his glance, B shrugged. "I know you love it."

"I do, thank you." He grabbed the rest of his grapes and put
them on Barclay's plate. "Ditto."

"Thank you." Barclay snapped up the grapes, then leaned back
in his chair. "That was very good. Thank you."

"It was, wasn't it? We did way better than we would have at the
restaurant. You're looking like you're feeling better too." Less like a
frozen ghost and more like his B.

"Yeah. I was startled, I guess."

"That's hardly surprising—you hadn't seen him in over a year."
He reached for Barclay's hand and took it, holding on. "You want to
move to the couches? They'll be more comfortable, and we can talk
to Union when he comes."

"Yeah." Barclay surprised him by locking his brakes and
standing on trembling legs. "Don't let me fall."

"Never." He slipped his arm around Barclay's waist. That way
he could catch Barclay immediately if necessary, but Barclay could
choose how much to lean on him as they walked over to the comfy
couches.

Barclay only misstepped once and caught himself. Then they made it to the couches.

Rec felt a little like cheering. Instead, he hugged Barclay tight and gave him a kiss. "That was amazing." Especially given the last hour or so.

"I've been practicing." There was a look of pride on Barclay's face.

While he was a little annoyed that Barclay had been practicing walking when he was home by himself—which had to be when he was doing it—he was also thrilled that Barclay had gotten this far on his own. "I'm very impressed." He totally was.

"Thank you. I want to be better, healthy, whole."

"I know. You're doing great too. I bet you're back in the three months you originally quoted me that I didn't think was possible." He was very proud of Barclay's tenaciousness.

There was a noise from the other side of the room, and he was immediately on the alert. The noise turned out to be Tide with a large man Rec had seen around the gym a time or two, but whom he'd never interacted with before. This had to be Union.

"Hey, y'all. What's up?" The big man came over, knelt down. "I'm Union. Pleased."

"Nice to meet you. Wish it was under better circumstances. I'm Reccc—call me Rec. And this is Barclay. He's having problems with his ex. You want to tell Union about it, B? Start at the beginning, with how you got injured." He took Barclay's hand, holding on and offering his support.

"He pushed me off the roof. I can't prove it, but I promise, I think he pushed me off the roof."

Union pulled his notebook out of his pocket, along with a pen, and started making notes. "When was this?"

Barclay explained the job, the weather, the four-story fall. "He was staring down at me and smiling. He was smiling at the hospital when he thought I was paralyzed. He was smiling at me today."

"That wasn't really a smile. It was an insane grimace." Rec shook his head. "He had those scary crazy eyes. You know? He's going to try something—try to hurt B again."

Union winced. "Have you got any evidence of any of this?"

"No."

Rec could see Barclay shrink, go tiny against the cushions.

"I'm sure you can do something, though," Rec insisted. He was going to push this as far as he had to.

"I can. Just not officially. If you have a picture of him, I can circulate it among the beat cops. Anyone sees him, they'll take note. If he's actively stalking you, we'll have it on file with our own guys as witnesses. I wish I could go arrest him, but without any evidence, we won't be able to keep him. But this will work. If we have eyes on him, he can't hurt you."

"I'm sure there's a picture of him, right, babe? Somewhere?" Although if it had been him, he probably would have gotten rid of any pictures after a breakup like that.

"Yeah. At my apartment. In my laptop."

"Your laptop's at the condo, B." He turned back to Union. "We can email you the picture as soon as we get home."

"So you're staying with Rec, but you've got your own place?" Union asked.

"Yeah. I mean, we're trying…. It's new, you know?"

"Good for you guys." Union smiled, looking honestly pleased for them. "Does your ex—what's his name?"

"Duncan Forsythe."

"Does Forsythe know you're living at Rec's now and not your apartment?"

Barclay frowned for a moment, then shook his head. "I don't think so? He said he kept knocking at the door."

"And he couldn't be doing that where you are now?" Union asked.

Rec shook his head. "We've got a security door that's locked. You either need to have a key or be buzzed up. B's place, you just walk in." His phone went off, but Rec sent the call to voicemail without even looking at who it was. This was more important right now.

"Okay, that's good." Union made another note in his book. "And we'll add your road to our patrol routes; a little extra police presence can't hurt."

"I'm not lying," Barclay whispered. "I swear to God."

"I believe you," Union said, looking Barclay in the eye. "But without evidence, we're screwed as far as what we can do. I could try and find him and intimidate him, but if I do that, he can accuse us of harassment. It'll be better for you if we wait until we have something concrete on him."

"Okay. I just want to be left alone, you know?" Barclay rubbed his thigh on his injured leg. "This has been hard enough."

Rec slipped his arm around Barclay's shoulders, offering him support.

"I can imagine. Was he your Dom?" Union asked.

"I didn't know what that was, not before Rec. He was… harsh."

"Did he abuse you?" Union was so gentle in his questioning.

"He tore out his nipple ring, man." That was abuse, right?

Union nodded and wrote that down. "Anything else? You said he was harsh?"

"He lost his temper with me. Hit me if I screwed up. You know."

Rec held Barclay tighter, pushing his anger away. He wasn't seeing red because of anything Barclay had done, and he needed to focus on being strong for Barclay right now. Letting his anger at Barclay's ex show wouldn't help any of them right now.

"Yeah, unfortunately I do know," Union said. "I'm sorry you went through that. If you wanted to send me a list of the things he's done to you via email as well, I'll get it added to the file."

"Yeah. Rec doesn't need to hear the details, right?"

"No, if you don't want to tell me, you don't have to. But if you need to talk about it, I'm here. No judgment. At least not of you." Rec wanted to know so he could help Barclay, but he totally didn't need to know if Barclay didn't want him to.

Barclay looked up at him. "I want you to see me like you always have, you know?"

"I wouldn't think less of you," Rec promised. "But I will totally abide by your wishes. I know you're a strong, wonderful man. You were when I met you—and you are now."

Barclay reached out for Rec, moving even closer. "Thank you. I'm glad. Thank you."

Rec gave Barclay a soft kiss, blocking everything else out for a moment. He leaned their foreheads together. "We'll get over this, and then he'll be gone and it'll just be you and me."

"You promise? I mean, I want it. I want to be yours."

"I'll tell you a secret, B. You already are mine."

Union hummed softly. "So sweet."

"Yeah, yeah. Just you wait—you'll be sweet yourself once day." He tucked Barclay against him and returned to more serious matters. "Is there anything else you need from us, Union?"

"Let me give you my card. Are you going to your apartment alone, Barclay?"

Rec answered that one without hesitation. "No."

"Good. Just in case, huh? You're at a significant disadvantage." Union pointed to Barclay's legs.

"I understand. I'll have to go and grab a few more things eventually, but not today." Barclay had already brought the essentials to his place.

"And you won't go alone when you do go back." Rec would be sure of that.

Barclay nodded for him, smiled tentatively. "I won't."

"Good." He turned back to Union. "Do you need anything else from us?"

"No. If I need anything else, I'll give you a call. Stay safe, okay?"

Rec nodded. He was going to make sure that happened.

Barclay sighed. "I'm sorry, Rec. I didn't mean to bring him into your life."

Rec didn't hesitate for a moment to answer. "This isn't your fault, B."

Union nodded. "He's right. The only person to blame in this is the stalker. I've seen more of these cases than I'd like to, and that holds true for all of them."

"Still, I wish... you know."

Rec leaned their heads together again. "I get that. But we found each other, and that's what I want to focus on."

"I found you, you mean." Oh, a tease! That had to mean Barclay was feeling more in control again.

Rec found himself grinning. "I might give you that."

Union chuckled and handed Rec the promised card. "Keep in touch."

He pocketed the card. "Yeah, you too. Please keep us updated on any developments."

Rec stood as Union did and shook the man's hand. B shook too and they were left alone, the big man wandering off.

He sat back with Barclay again and sighed. "Well, I think that went as well as it could have. How are you feeling?" Rec could see from Barclay's color that he was doing much better now.

"I feel a little silly, a lot cared for."

"You shouldn't feel silly. Your reactions were all valid." That pretty much went for everything. Feelings were what they were.

"Who was your call from?" Barclay asked.

"Oh, right." He'd forgotten about it. Grabbing his phone, he checked his recent calls. "It was the clinic. They left a message." Excitement went through him. He was looking forward to good results for both of them. God, this was turning out to be an up-and-down day.

Barclay paled again. "Please. Please let it be okay."

He took Barclay's hand and squeezed yet again, holding tight. "No matter what they say, it's going to be okay. I promise." He hit the voicemail and Play.

"Good morning, Mr. Gordon, this is the Applebee Clinic. Both tests that you are the contact for came back negative. There's no reason for you to come in and see the doctor unless you have questions. Thank you."

"Oh." Barclay took a huge breath. "Oh yay."

He laughed and hugged Barclay close. "We're both fine." Then he leaned in and whispered into Barclay's ear. "When we get home, I'm going to make love to you bareback, and then I'm going to plug you with my seed still inside you."

"I—" Barclay jerked against him, shivered. "You…. You're going to make me ache."

"That's a good thing, B. I think it would be fun if you're hard all the trip home. It's okay—I'll push you so you can put your hands over your erection."

"Rec!" That laugh sounded so good. So fucking good to him.

"What?" he asked, keeping his eyes wide, like he didn't have a clue.

"You're evil." Barclay grabbed him and kissed him hard. "Thank you for sticking with me, for all your support."

"I'm not a fair-weather friend, B. I care about you, more every day. Thank you for trusting me and staying." He rubbed their noses together.

"More every day," Barclay repeated, licking at Rec's lips.

His own cock began to fill, and it made him smile—he was going to need to push Barclay so the wheelchair hid *his* erection.

Barclay licked his lips again, tracing his smile, grinning at him when he was done. That expression—it went right up to Barclay's eyes—made Rec so happy.

"I love you," he said softly, the words sliding from his lips as easy as you please. He'd never told anyone that before, except for his parents.

"Yeah?" Barclay searched his eyes. "I'm in the same boat somehow."

"You are?" He beamed, holding Barclay's gaze. "Because that makes it so much better. Like, so much." And it was pretty damn good just loving Barclay.

"I am. And I think so too. So much."

Laughing with his happiness, he pressed their mouths together, taking the happiest kiss he'd ever shared.

There was a noise at the other end of the room again, and he pulled out of the kiss, resting his forehead against Barclay's for a moment. Then he looked up.

Tide came toward them, an apologetic smile on his face. "I don't want to interrupt anything, but I wanted to make sure everything was okay up here."

"Yeah, Union is a star, and I'm keeping Barclay close, just in case."

"Good deal. We've checked the street. He's not out there right now, so if you wanted to go, it's a good time. Not that you have to, of course. You can stay as long as you need to."

Rec shook his head. "No, we're going to head home." He met Barclay's gaze, smiling.

"I want to go home. I'll pay for a cab even."

"We can walk home. It's not far, and the guys checked—he's gone." Rec leaned in to whisper again. "I meant it about wanting you aching all the way home, though. So once Tide leaves, I'm going to make you quite hard."

"Be nice!" Barclay sounded shocked.

"What? I'm being very nice!"

Tide chuckled at them, but turned and headed away without saying a word.

"See? Tide was embarrassed!"

"He was not! He was giving you privacy because he's a Dom and he probably knew what kind of thing we were talking about. What kind of thing I might have planned."

"Totally embarrassed." Barclay's eyes were dancing.

"Cheeky!" He laughed and went for Barclay's ribs, digging his fingers in to tickle. He was loving this more playful side of Barclay. It was like now that they'd faced Forsythe, now that he and others had taken Barclay at his word, a weight had been lifted.

He had no doubt that the worry would come back, but he'd take this for now.

Chapter Nine

Barclay wasn't going to be scared.

He wasn't.

They were heading home, and he wasn't going to stare and worry and watch, dammit.

He was going to be with his lover.

He wasn't fully erect, but Rec had kept his promise and he was hard, his hands lying casually in his lap so it wouldn't be noticed as Rec pushed his chair.

They were both negative, and that was so much better to focus on than anything else. That and the promises Rec had made him for what was going to happen when they got home.

They got to the front doors and he used his key—his key!—to let them into the lobby. Rec wheeled him right to the elevator, and he pressed the button.

"Feels like it's taking forever to get there," Rec noted after a moment.

"Yeah, but the anticipation doesn't suck either, huh?" It was like a constant sweet buzz.

"Yep. You're learning. And now you know why I wanted you hard for our trip home." Rec sounded smug. Deservedly so.

"You just like me needing you." He got it. He knew Rec was doing the same, needing him.

"That's definitely a part of it. I'm also having a hard time keeping my own cock under control. I can't wait to make love to you. Just you and me, and maybe a little lube." Rec laughed, the sound a little wild and a lot eager.

"Yeah. You won't have to pull out. You can stay in."

"Mmm. You know I've been looking forward to falling asleep still buried inside you. It's something I've always wanted to do."

The elevator finally showed, and Rec pushed him on, pressed the button for their floor.

He wanted to jack off, rub himself, but he knew that Rec didn't want him to, wanted him to wait.

Rec stood next to him, shooting him a grin. "Won't be long now." The anticipation danced across Rec's face.

"Nope. Just a few floors, that's all." He shivered with excitement.

Rec's hand slid over his shoulder, the connection, simple as it was, positively electric. He gasped softly, his ass sliding on the chair cushion.

The elevator came to a smooth stop, and Rec pushed him out, moving quickly down the hall with his chair. "Open the door to our home, B."

"Our home. It seems... like a dream." He reached out and put the key in the lock—put his key in the lock—and turned the knob.

Rec didn't linger once he had the door open, and that eagerness was both gratifying and infectious, ramping up his need.

"Bed, huh? Us? Together, in bed?"

"Uh-huh. You and me and a date with my cock and your ass." Rec laughed. "Sorry, I'm feeling a little giddy."

"That's exciting. The giddy. I keep wanting to jack myself off."

"Oh no. No jacking off. In fact, I think we should make that a rule, eh? No jacking off. No touching that lovely cock of yours without my permission." Rec moved them into the bedroom.

"Are there usually rules?"

"Yeah, there often are. But every couple makes their own rules. Decides their own punishments. It's the same as the plugs—they are for enjoyment and for pushing, stretching the boundaries. It's meant to make things more intense for both of us. Better."

"I—I don't know...." God, he was buzzing.

"Oh, I think you know enough." Rec crouched next to him, hand sliding across his lap to grab his package. He spread, his thighs going tight, hard.

"It's going to be so hot—knowing that you're going to have to wait for my touch on your cock." Rec pulled Barclay's shirt out of his sweats, baring his belly, making him shiver.

Bending, Rec pressed his lips against Barclay's belly, the kiss soft and warm, full of promise and right there near his needy cock.

"I—I want you. Bad." His fingers tightened on the arm of the chair.

"Me too." Rec ducked his chin, rubbing Barclay's cock through his sweats, making him moan and try to buck. It was awkward in the chair, though. "Let's get you out of this chair." Rec stood and offered his hands, smiling down at him.

"Good thing it wasn't leg day." Barclay held on and stood on legs that were getting stronger and stronger.

"I don't think it would have mattered. Just look at you." There was pride in Rec's voice. "You're going to be showing me what you can do in no time on all."

He was sure as hell going to try. "Later. Now I want to make love. Please."

"God yes." Rec drew him close, arms wrapping around his waist. Those hands held and supported him, and he didn't worry about falling as Rec kissed him, stealing his sense and his breath. He wanted to simply melt against Rec.

They shuffled to the bedroom, slowly and steadily, kissing the entire way. Rec made sure he didn't fall, and by the time they were by the bed, he was fully hard, his clothing irritating his skin. He needed it off.

Rec seemed to be reading his mind, and he raised Barclay's T-shirt up over his head, pulling it away. The sudden cool air made him shiver, but Rec's hands were all over him, hot and arousing.

"More. Please, that's good. More." He pushed his sweats down.

"How about me?" Rec asked, pointing to his own shirt and workout shorts. "I need to be naked too."

"God yes. All of you. Please." He yanked at Rec's shirt, fingers tearing at the cloth.

"That's right." Rec lifted his arms, letting Barclay pull the T-shirt up and off.

Then he yanked at Rec's shorts. Rec helped him get them off, then got the rest of Barclay's sweats off. Taking a half step back, Rec looked him from top to bottom and licked his lips. "I can't decide which I want to do more—pounce you and fuck you blind, or make it last."

"Can't we do both? Please?" He lay down on his belly and put his ass in the air.

Rec groaned for him and climbed up, cock burning hot as it rubbed against his ass. "Yes. Pouncing first, lasting second."

"Perfect. Perfect plan." Barclay wanted it. He wanted to be taken, fucked. Loved.

Leaning over him, Rec reached past him to grab the lube. Barclay almost wanted to tell Rec to skip the lube and just fuck him, but then Rec's slick finger pushed into him and it felt so good. He pushed back into the invasion, and Rec fingerfucked him with just that one finger, warming him from the inside. He rocked back and forth, riding it before he couldn't wait longer and asked for more.

"Two now." Rec pushed two fingers into him, pushing them deep enough to touch his gland. Everything inside him lit up, the touches exciting.

It all seemed bigger too, with the specter of this being the first time they were going without a condom hanging there, painting it all with an extra layer of excitement. His cock throbbed, and he spread a little wider, his balls swinging.

Rec didn't use two fingers for very long. He soon pushed in another finger, spreading Barclay even wider. Those three fingers worked him well as Rec whispered "love" and "God" and "baby boy," voice rough with need.

"Yours. Don't stop. I need you."

"Not stopping. Wanna be buried inside you." Rec drew his fingers away, and then Barclay felt the heat of Rec's cock against his skin. There wasn't any wait for a condom, just that blunt heat. Skin on skin.

"I can feel you." Rec's skin on his skin.

"I sure hope you can." Rec rubbed his cockhead along Barclay's hole—back and forth.

He wanted more. He needed more, and he pushed back impatiently. Rec laughed and rubbed one more time before driving against him, breaching his hole. His body stretched, accepting Rec eagerly.

He swore he could feel the difference without the condom, the heat unbelievable, burning his ass up in the best damn way. He knew he could hear the difference—Rec's moans were insane and pretty much constant.

Rec moved in and out again, the first few times long and slow. Then Rec's forehead dropped onto his back, and the thrusts got stronger, quicker, giving him what he'd so badly wanted. He rocked back, meeting every plunge in, driving them together again and again.

"B. B. B." Over and over, Rec called out his name, cock driving into him, gliding in, slick and silky, pure, wonderful heat.

"Yeah...." He bore down, clenching hard.

Rec's hands wrapped around his waist, fingers digging in how he liked it, hard enough to leave marks. With every thrust, Rec pulled him back, helping him move into the invasion.

The pleasure built and built, driving his need higher.

"Gonna," he warned. "Soon." He wanted to feel Rec coming in him, filling him up, marking him inside.

"Yeah. Fuck yeah." Rec slid a hand beneath him and grabbed his cock. "So tight, B. You're perfect. Perfect." Rec's movements became almost frantic, driving into him without rhyme or reason now, which could only mean Rec was close too. "Do it! Come on my cock, baby!"

The wild words pushed him over the edge, leaving him dazed, needy. He felt it, though, felt it as Rec slammed in one more time and filled him with heat. It shot deep inside him, Rec's cock pulsing. Rec collapsed onto him with a groan.

He collapsed onto the mattress in turn, letting Rec cover him, surround him. Soft kisses dropped onto his skin, lazy and easy. Hot. In fact, that was the word of the day. Rec surrounded him with heat.

"Wow." It was the best he could do, the most he had.

"Uh-huh." More kisses spread across his neck. The best, though, was that Rec stayed right there inside him, buried deep and filling him. Filling him right up, hot and good and right.

He groaned and let his eyes fall closed as he focused on the afterglow, the pleasure.

Rec's touches were lazy, fingers sliding across his skin randomly. Every now and then he'd murmur, not even words, just sounds that were sweet as honey. Barclay floated easily, tightening his ass every so often.

"Gonna keep me hard," Rec told him, like it was a warning. Or maybe it was a promise.

"That's okay. I can live with that."

"Yeah, so can I." Rec chuckled, the sound husky and deep. "After all, I did promise you to make it last after we went for it. Gonna stay in a bit longer, then I'll do you for as long as I can."

"Mmm. You can stay as long as you want."

"Feels good, doesn't it? I'm really glad we did this—got tested, I mean. This is really nice, being held by your body." Rec hugged him, fingers lingering on his belly, warming him down deep.

"Uh-huh. It's been the best news."

"Yeah. I love that you wanted this too." Rec danced his fingers up toward Barclay's nipples, moving slowly like he had all the time in the world to build the anticipation.

His body tightened as he waited, his world closing down to a space where nothing existed but his ass and his nips. When Rec finally reached his right, unscarred nipple, the light brush of fingertips felt enormous, absolutely huge, and he clenched, his ass squeezing Rec tight.

Rec's low groan was almost a touch, and it made him shiver. "Do that again, baby. Squeeze me."

He was more than happy to comply, and he clenched again. Rec's heat inside him felt amazing, and the way Rec kept touching his nipple made it feel more intense. When Rec's fingers drifted over to trace the scars on his left nipple, it had his anticipation building again.

"Have you considered another piercing? Something new?"

He shook his head. "I hadn't, no."

"I think you'd look sexy. Either a hoop in both, or a barbell in one, a hoop in the other. It would let me tug more easily." After tracing his scars, Rec plucked at his nipple, pulling it gently from his chest.

"Oh." He arched, ass pushing back into Rec.

"Mmm. You ready to move again?" Rec rolled his hips, moving the thick cock inside him without thrusting. It caused Rec's cockhead to brush against his gland, sending a shiver of pleasure through his entire body. At the same time, Rec tugged on his nipple again.

Barclay cried out, the sound echoing against the headboard.

"Love the noises you make. I like that I can tell if you're getting off on what I'm doing." Rec dropped soft kisses on his shoulder and neck, lips warm, the kisses leaving damp spots on his skin. Another circle of Rec's hips sent an additional shiver of pleasure throughout his body.

"Jesus. God, don't stop. That's magic."

"This?" Rec circled his hips again. "Or this?" That gentle tug to his nipple was repeated. "Or this?" Rec laid a few more kisses on his skin.

"Yes!"

Rec chuckled, but he didn't stop anything he'd been doing. Thank God.

"Laughing at me," he teased.

"With you, B. Totally with you. I've never had an experience like this." Rec groaned as he rolled his hips, then again, finding a slow rhythm that Barclay was convinced was designed to drive him absolutely crazy with pleasure.

Tug and thrust and pull and push. He was going to lose his mind. Rec's kisses and the sounds coming from him were the final pieces to make it all perfect. He was hard again too, his cock leaving wet spots on his belly. Even without Rec touching it at all.

"Making me so crazy, Rec."

"Good." Rec laughed, nuzzling his cheek. "That's what I want. Crazy from pleasure." Rec sped his movements, thrusting more than circling his hips now. It ratcheted everything else up.

"Yes. Crazy from pleasure. From you." He burned, his ass full, his body buzzing.

"Wanna do this all day." Rec was crazy, but Barclay had to admit, he liked the idea and he was up for trying.

"I'm in. I want to play for days."

"Good thing it's Friday, then. We have days before either of us has to be anywhere but right here in bed." Rec bit at his earlobe, the pain unexpected, sharp, then soothed by Rec sucking on it.

Days. God yes. He wanted this. Rec. Now.

Rec increased the speed and strength of his thrusts, not enough to send him over yet, but enough to keep him gasping and moaning, his hands opening and closing in the bedding. "We're not in a hurry, baby. Breathe."

Breathe. Right. It sounded a lot easier than it was with his entire body focused on Rec, on the pleasure.

"I could stop for a bit," Rec suggested, although he hadn't yet. "Give you a moment to catch your breath."

"Don't stop…." It was so good.

"I wasn't going to—just teasing you." Rec groaned, proving that he was affected too. That he wanted this as much as Barclay did. Even if he did have enough brain power left to tease.

He focused on working Rec's cock, on milking him rhythmically. Rec made this sound, a drawn-out moan that was entirely obscene and ran right down his spine. His lover was the sexiest man on the planet, no doubt about it.

The way he affected Rec made him feel about twenty feet tall.

They continued to move together, and the pleasure built, wrapping around both of them. Nothing else existed. No one else existed. Right here in bed was all there was.

Rec's lips pressed against his neck, the caress gentle and warm, making him shiver. He wanted to kiss Rec in return, but that wouldn't work with the way they were lying. He grabbed Rec's hand and brought it up to his mouth, his lips sliding across Rec's palm. Rec gasped for him, the soft sound sending a rush of air against his skin. Oh yes. He sucked in one finger, humming over the digit, lashing it with his tongue.

"Fuck that's good." Rec pushed in harder, nailing his gland this time and lighting him up in a much bigger way.

He dragged his teeth along Rec's finger, enough to make it sting.

"B! Fuck! Yes!" Rec punched in again, keeping the strength right there with every thrust.

The way they were moving together was intoxicating, and Barclay cried out over and over, his heart slamming in his chest. This was everything.

He floated on that thought and the sensations building and building between them. He had no idea how long they were at it, how long it lasted. It didn't matter. All that did matter was this, right here in their bed. Rec's cock in his ass, the love between them.

The way the world seemed to pulsate, nice and slow.

Everything disappeared, and he was in this haze with Rec.

When his orgasm came, it was a surprise, the pleasure huge and moving through him from his balls to his cock, rushing like waves over his body.

It pulsed, over and over, and he trusted in it, in Rec.

By the time the last aftershocks had rippled through him, he was totally limp. Rec breathed heavily behind him, panting against his shoulder. A low moan sounded, and Rec managed to squeeze him gently. "So good."

"Uh-huh. Love." Better than good.

"Mmm. I love you, Barclay." Rec smiled against his skin. "Time for that nap while I'm still buried inside you."

"Yeah." He was melted, mostly asleep, and simply toast. He could get used to this. He wanted to get used to this.

"Sleep," muttered Rec. "Now."

He agreed. Maybe. Or not.

It didn't matter, Barclay was asleep.

Chapter Ten

REC PULLED the van they'd borrowed off Ian—one of the gym members—up in front of Barclay's building. They were here to get the rest of Barclay's stuff. His boy was moving in for good. Barclay had already put in his notice on the apartment.

He turned to Barclay and grinned. "You ready to close out this chapter of your life?"

"I am. There's not much. Some clothes, photos, artwork." Barclay was out of the chair these days, using his crutches to stabilize himself.

"It's yours, though. And the condo will feel more like ours instead of just mine when we've got your bits and pieces there." He got out and went around to open Barclay's door and be there if his boy needed any help getting down out of the higher seat.

Barclay held his arms, balancing and easing down before getting his crutches. "I'm getting better."

"You so are. I'm going to get to watch you running that ninja course at the gym in no time." He was looking forward to it. He was going to pick Barclay's brains for the ninja training class he was going to run for the gym.

"If it was all upper-body stuff, I'd be kicking ass."

"You need your legs to kick ass, B." He bit his lip to keep from laughing and ruining the joke.

"Uh-huh. I will beat you."

"Nope. I'm the Dom—that's my job. If that was our kink." They were into fucking and filling and comfort and care. A little bondage.

His boy didn't need pain. They needed their connection, to stretch together.

He followed Barclay into the building. That way he got to watch Barclay's ass. It was a great view. Barclay managed to make it down to his apartment at the end of the hall without a single hitch. Then he stood there, staring at the door.

"Not having second thoughts, are you?"

Barclay shook his head and pointed at the door. Which was already open.

He immediately grabbed his boy and moved him back. No. No way. "Let me call Union."

"But this is my place, Rec."

"Yeah, and we'll go in when Union gets here." He got Barclay turned around and moving back down the hall. "We'll wait in the van." Just in case that asshole was still in there.

"But...."

He was going to pick Barclay up and carry him. "Please, baby. For me. Please."

Barclay looked at him, then nodded. "Okay. Okay, sure. For you."

"Good." He followed Barclay back out and opened the van door for him. When he got around to his side and both doors were closed, he locked them. Then he called Union.

"Yo, what's up, man?" Union always sounded like he was nearly asleep.

"Barclay's apartment's been broken into. We just got here and the door is open. We didn't go in. I don't know if he's still there." They had to send someone now.

"On my way. Do not go in."

"No, we're back in the van. We're parked out front, doors locked."

"Good. Smart. Give me five." Then the line went dead.

"What did he say?"

"He's on his way and don't go in." He took Barclay's hand. "He's on it. They're taking this very seriously." He took a deep breath. "They'll have a reason to bring him in after this. That's breaking and entering."

"What if he's in there? What if he's messing with my stuff?"

"Then Union is going to arrest him and take him to jail." As long as Barclay himself was okay, Rec didn't think some stuff was that big of a sacrifice. And maybe that wasn't fair, because it wasn't his stuff.

Still, he would replace everything so long as his Barclay was safe. In the end, that was all that counted.

"What did you think of Union?" The big man was a sub, though he'd bet no one would guess that from seeing him. The guy was huge.

"He's been very kind. I mean, seriously."

"Really gentle for such a big guy," Rec added. Someone came out of Barclay's building, and he narrowed his eyes until he realized it was a woman. He relaxed.

"Big doesn't mean 'mean,' you know?"

"No, I know that. He's a great example of don't judge a book by its cover."

"Yeah, that seems like it's always a thing, doesn't it? Being judgy fucks you."

He nodded and glanced at his watch. *Come on Union*, he thought. *Let's get here and get this guy.*

The police car pulled up behind them, and Rec jumped out to tell them which apartment was B's. Union pulled up behind the police car.

"Back in your vehicle." Union pointed, and Rec nodded, moving back into the van.

Barclay was gathering his crutches, a determined look on his face.

"Where do you think you're going?" He was not letting Barclay anywhere near where his ex might be.

"This is my place! My fault."

"It might be your place, but this is in no way your fault. Your ex is crazy, and what he does is on him. Not you."

"Still. God. This is crazy, man. I want to get my shit."

"As soon as we know it's safe, right? You are worth more than anything you own. Anything. Any. Thing." It was worth repeating. He reached out and took Barclay's hand, squeezed it tight. "I mean it, boy. I need you."

"Oh." Barclay clung to his hand, looking pleased at his words.

It constantly surprised him how Barclay craved the slightest praise. It made him a little sad that Barclay so clearly hadn't had a lot of it in his past. And maybe angry. Of course, part of that was his anger at the ex too.

He took a breath and found a smile for Barclay. "This is the last time you're going to need to be here. You're officially coming home."

"Yes. I'm coming home. To stay."

"Yeah." That made him so happy. He leaned over and brought their mouths together, giving Barclay a kiss that held his entire focus. Nothing else mattered right at this moment. Barclay returned the kiss eagerly. Cupping Barclay's cheeks when the kiss was over, he rested their foreheads together and they breathed as one.

His timing was good, because as he sat back, he saw Union and the two uniformed policemen coming out of the apartment building. The uniforms made their way back to their car while Union came to him and Barclay. He climbed out and went around to open Barclay's door, figuring that Barclay could sit where he was while Union gave them the lowdown. It was obvious that Forsythe hadn't been there anymore.

Union looked serious, and he gave them both a terse nod. "The place is trashed. I've got a forensics team coming. With any luck, we'll find fingerprints. Have you ever had him over, Barclay?"

"No. Never. I didn't even know he knew where I lived until the other day when he said he'd been knocking and I hadn't been answering."

Rec put his arm around Barclay and rubbed his back. This sucked big-time.

"Can I go in? I need to get my stuff." Barclay asked.

"I'm not sure how much is salvageable, but I'd like you to wait until the forensics team is done. That way you don't taint any evidence. You'll be able to come back tomorrow."

Barclay sighed.

"It's okay, B. We'll come back and get your stuff tomorrow." He poured as much comfort as he could through his hands.

"There's not a whole lot that wasn't destroyed," Union noted. "It's pretty bad. What's not broken has been peed on. You might be better off hiring a company to come in and clear the place out, then deep clean it. You probably don't want to see it."

"I think I need to." Barclay turned to Rec. "I need to see what happened. To know. Does that make me crazy?"

Rec shook his head. "No. No, it doesn't. It means you need some closure, and if this gives it to you, then I'm behind you a hundred percent." He would always be behind Barclay. Always.

Barclay squeezed his hand. "Thank you." Then he turned to Union. "I'd like to see, please. I won't touch anything, but I'm imagining all sorts of stuff, and if I see it, then I'll know and I can.... Well, then I'll know."

"That's your prerogative, of course. Come on, I'll bring you in—we've put police tape across the door, but we can duck under it. I'd like to have a copy of your key so we can lock the door behind us. We can go get one cut after you look around."

"Okay."

Rec made sure Barclay made it down from the van, then followed behind him again. This time it was to protect him should the ex suddenly appear. With him and Union as escorts, Forsythe would be crazy to try to go for Barclay. Of course that was half the problem, wasn't it—Barclay's ex was off his rocker.

When they got to Barclay's door, Union turned and gave them each a direct look. "It's not a nice sight. Are you sure?"

"I have to know," Barclay insisted.

"And I'm not letting him confront it on his own," Rec added. He would be there for Barclay, no question.

Barclay grabbed his hand for a minute and held on tight. Then he took a deep breath and grabbed the handles of his crutches. "I'm ready."

Union held back the tape and Barclay ducked beneath it, Rec right behind him. Rec nearly bowled Barclay over when he stopped right inside the door, a small gasp coming from him. "Oh my God."

"I don't think God had anything to do with this." Rec looked around at the destruction; he thought this kind of thing only happened in the movies.

The television was on the floor, the glass shattered into thousands of pieces. The one bookshelf had been emptied out, books torn up, photos ripped apart, the frames bent, glass broken and scattered everywhere. The mattress had been torn open, a knife still sticking out of it at one end, and it was wet, the smell confirming that the liquid was piss. All the cupboards were open, several of their doors torn off their hinges, and food was smeared all over the wall.

The word "bitchy-poo" was written in what Rec hoped was ketchup across one wall and "kill you" covered the one opposite.

There was clearly nothing in here to be salvaged. Nothing at all.

Rec stepped up close to Barclay, being a wall at his back. "I'm so sorry, B." This was a horrible invasion—a personal attack no matter that the things broken and violated were just that—things. He didn't want to think what would have happened if Barclay had been here for this. Forsythe had tried to kill him once already, after all.

"He's actually done us a favor," Union noted as he entered the little apartment. "We can arrest him for the breaking in and the vandalism. He's left his DNA on the mattress, and I'm willing to bet we'll find fingerprints too. And that"—Union pointed at the threat on the far wall—"is a direct threat to you. Now we can detain him and test his DNA to confirm it's a match."

"Some favor," muttered Barclay.

Union nodded sympathetically. "I know it doesn't seem that way, but if he'd just kept following you, we couldn't have done anything about it, and it might have escalated to this kind of rage against you directly. This way we can act before it comes to that."

"I know. I just…. It's going to take some time for me to find the good in this."

"That's fair." Rec rubbed circles on Barclay's back, hoping to offer comfort. "Come on, let's go home. We'll hire someone to clean this place up and ask them to put aside anything they find that's worth salvaging. You don't have to deal with this."

Barclay nodded stiffly and turned around, the look on his face quiet and determined. He ducked under the police tape and headed back down the hall. Rec followed.

Barclay didn't say a word all the way back to the van, and Rec respected his quiet. He helped Barclay back up into the van, then went around to the driver's side.

"You okay?"

"I don't know. I mean, I…. It's not like anything I had was worth anything, but I had some books, some pictures, and a couple trophies that really meant something to me, and now they're gone. Like gone, gone. Destroyed. What did I do to make him hate me so badly?"

"I don't know, baby." How did he answer that? "I honestly think he's not all there. He's crazy, and that hasn't got anything to do with you. I think you're just a convenient target to him. I'm just grateful you weren't there when he showed up."

Barclay shivered. "Yeah, me too. I almost came by myself."

"You know I was never going to let you do that. Not after we ran into him in the street a couple weeks ago. Let me take you home. I'll even pick up some powdered doughnuts at the grocers on the corner."

Barclay's mouth quirked up into a smile at the mention of doughnuts. Score.

"Maybe I'll smear them all over your body so I can lick the sugar off your skin. Hell, maybe I'll smear them all over *my* body. Tempt you into eating me up."

"You don't need doughnuts for that, Rec." Barclay glanced up at him, that smile remaining on his face. "I'll gladly eat you any day."

"Woo! Well, then, why are we still parked here? I need to get you home so we can drop trou and get to munching."

Barclay's laughter was one of his favorite sounds in the world, and he almost didn't want to start up the engine and cover it up.

"Take me home already," Barclay told him.

"Yes, Boss." He grinned as he started up the engine, ducking Barclay's halfhearted swat. This was much better than moping or getting depressed over the loss of what were just things in the end. They would find new stuff that was important to them together.

They wound up taking the van to the gym when a quick text proved that Ian was still there, finishing up his workout. Rec suspected that he'd actually hooked up with a sub for some afternoon delight, but he didn't say anything. They left the van in the parking lot and the keys with the front desk, then headed back out.

"Are you going to be okay walking all the way back? We could Uber it." He probably should have driven Barclay home before dropping off the van, but he hadn't wanted to leave Barclay there by himself. Forsythe was still out there, and for all they knew, the guy had been sitting in a car staking out Barclay's old place, waiting to follow them.

"I want to try." Barclay had that stubborn set to his face he got whenever Rec suggested cutting his workout short for whatever reason. It was that determination that had brought Barclay this far this quickly, and Rec had no doubt Barclay was going to make it back. There might be a soak in the tub and a massage needed at the end of it, but his money was on Barclay walking the entire kilometer home.

He fell into step with Barclay, the sunshine warm on their backs. "You want any water?" he asked as they passed the little grocers at the end of their street. He'd promised to pick up powdered doughnuts.

"Yeah, actually. I could use some."

They went in together and traveled up and down the aisles, grabbing the doughnuts, a loaf of bread, and some cheese, along with some juice and the bottle of water they'd originally come in for. Rec found himself glancing around and checking out the other patrons, making sure none of them were Barclay's ex.

He hated that, hated that he was paranoid now and looking for evil lurking around corners. They needed to be vigilant, though, until Forsythe got picked up.

They paid for the stuff and stood under the awning outside the store, munching on a couple doughnuts and drinking most of the water between them. Then they continued on, Barclay seeming to have caught a second wind from their pit stop.

"You want to talk about it?" Rec asked.

"Not really. I mean, it's done. The most important stuff was already moved, I guess. I'm sad for the few things I lost that were important to me, but it's not like anyone died or anyone was hurt. This time." Barclay sighed, rolled his shoulders. "I just want... I don't know. I want things to be okay."

He thought about that as they walked, the bag swinging against his leg rhythmically. "Well. Things between you and me are going awesome. Your rehabilitation is coming along great. I think if you put everything together, we're doing better than okay."

"That's an interesting way of thinking about things." Barclay stopped, panting some. They were a little over halfway there. "Is there any more water left?"

He passed it over. "Go ahead and finish it. We have juice too. If you need a longer break, there's the bench by the bus stop."

"I'm fine. I am. I just…. I'm fine." Barclay sucked the water down.

He wasn't entirely sure having Barclay walk home the rest of the way was the best decision, but he also knew his lover was going to tough it out and make it happen. That tenacity was a part of why he loved Barclay. "Okay. Fine, boy, let's keep going."

"I am. Don't push. I'm going. I've had a bit of a day."

"I know, B. And I'm not the one pushing—you are. You're going to do it too. And I promise a massage and a hot bath when we get home." He couldn't wait to get his hands all over Barclay. It might have only been this morning since they last touched, but he was eager like it had been much longer than that.

He knew a part of it was needing to make sure that Barclay was all right. He needed to spend time connecting deeply.

"You're doing great," he told Barclay when his boy appeared to be lagging. "We're almost there, and I'm warming my fingers up to give you a massage." He held out his hands so Barclay could see as he opened and closed his fingers.

Barclay laughed for him, which was what he'd been going for. Excellent. Buoyed by the laughter, they easily made it the last hundred meters. Rec let them in, and Barclay crutched his way to the elevator, which was already on the ground floor waiting for them. They went in, and Barclay leaned against the back wall with a sigh.

"You made it." Rec pressed the button for their floor.

"Almost—I still have to get down the hall. And then to the bedroom."

"Taking your massage on the bed rather than the couch?"

"That'll be more comfortable for what comes after the massage," Barclay noted.

"A nap?"

"Eventually, sure. But not what I'm hoping for."

Happiness surged through his body, and he smiled at Barclay. "I think maybe that can be arranged."

"I thought so." Barclay sounded slightly smug but mostly happy, and that worked for Rec.

The elevator came to a stop and he went down the hall with his boy. Going home together.

Chapter Eleven

BARCLAY WAS helping Rec put together a ninja warrior class. While he couldn't really do the balance or leg-intensive obstacles yet, he rocked the upper-body and finger-strength ones, so he could demonstrate those and explain how the others worked and suggest where they should be slotted within the coursework.

They decided on two evenings a week for the course, where each evening would focus on two or three of the obstacles. The courses were twelve weeks long, and the last two weeks would put everything together. It was designed to have everyone ready to run an obstacle-course race by the time they were done.

It felt so good to have something to do again. To be useful. He was even getting paid for "consulting," and Tyrone had told him that if the course was popular, they'd add a second one next year, and if he was up to it, he could teach it. There was even the possibility there'd be interest in one during the day or on weekends.

Barclay and Rec leaned over Rec's iPad, finalizing the course plan.

"You know, it'd be great to have you help me out with this," Rec suggested. "I'll give you half of what they're paying me to be my assistant."

"I still have savings," he pointed out. He didn't need charity.

"It isn't about making sure you have money. I think you'll lend veracity to the course, being a stuntman and all, so that should increase sign-ups. And if you're assisting me and working the same hours I am, it's only fair you get some of the credit and money. If you don't want to do it, that's another story. You can just say so, though."

"No, I want to do it." Working with Rec on the planning over the last couple of days proved how much he wanted to be doing things again, doing more than just his physical therapy. He needed an outlet. This one seemed ideal. And he liked the Iron Eagle's clientele. Everyone had been welcoming, had treated him like one of their own.

He'd even spoken with some of the subs, and most of them were happy to share their experiences with him. Hell, Lance and Bran had all but taken him under their wings. Lance was a sweetheart, and Bran had a wicked sense of humor and could have a sharp tongue, but you could tell he was a good guy. They made him feel like he belonged even if he wasn't into spanking and whips and shit. Apparently not everyone who was into BDSM was. It was rather fascinating.

Rec poked him in the side.

Barclay frowned. "What was that for?"

"You're woolgathering."

He looked down at his hands. "Nope. No wool."

Rec laughed and Barclay watched. He loved how happiness looked on Rec's face.

"Seriously, what were you thinking about?" Rec asked.

Barclay lifted one shoulder in a shrug. "About Lance and Bran and how different we all are. How that's cool."

He'd seen some things at the gym that did nothing for him, but that was cool. He got that. Hell, he liked it. It made him feel that Rec needed what he had and vice versa.

"That's one of the really cool things about the lifestyle. It caters to everyone no matter their kinks. There's lots of stuff I'm surprised folks are into, but to each their own. You know? And as a community everyone is really accepting."

"At least they pretend to be." He knew that there were bad seeds in every community, people that were mean or intolerant, what have you. There were good and bad people in every kind of community.

"I think Lance and Bran are being honestly friendly in their overtures to you," Rec noted. "The subs especially seem to be pleased whenever they have a new member of their community."

"Oh, I think so too. Totally. They've been great. I mean, in general. Just because someone's kinky doesn't mean they're good."

"Ah, I get what you mean. And you're right, of course. There's bad people in any subset of people." Once again, Rec echoed his thoughts. That happened a lot, and Barclay liked it. It made it feel like they were on the same wavelength.

Rec made a few changes on the last page of the course info before handing the iPad over. "There. What do you think?"

He looked it over and nodded, satisfied with the plan. "I think this will be fun, don't you?" Fun, but also instructional. It would be hard for the participants, but if they put in the work, they'd come out fit, capable, and prepared to participate competently in obstacle races.

"I do. I bet the course is going to fill up fast, and they'll add another one when this one has run its course. Maybe even split them into intermediate and beginner, something like that." Rec saved the chart and emailed it to the guys who were on the board for the gym. "We should get official feedback on Monday, but Tyrone was pretty sure this class out of all of them would be the one that we got enough people for, hands down."

Rec was excited about the courses, he could tell. He liked the enthusiasm, the energy. It lit Rec up from the inside.

"You ready for some lunch?" Rec asked.

He was.

"I need to hit the head, so I'll meet you up front." Rec leaned in and gently brushed their lips together.

"Sounds good." Barclay grabbed his crutches and headed to the front. They were just there for balance and safety these days. It was a gorgeous day out, so he went outside to wait for Rec in the sunshine. He raised his head to soak in the sun, when he was suddenly thrown into shadow.

He shielded his eyes, Duncan coming into view, his ex standing over him.

"You don't belong here. I will call the cops." He had his crutches in hand; he could beat Duncan down if he had to.

"Oh, Bitchy-poo grew a spine." How had he never noticed before how whiny and scratchy Duncan's voice was?

"Fuck off, you moron." He hadn't ever been scared of Duncan, more stunned by his reputation, astonished at the abuse, and then ashamed.

"What did you say to me?" Duncan looked shocked, like honestly shocked.

"I said, fuck off, you moron. Do you need me to use smaller words?"

Duncan took a step back. Then his expression turned mean, and he made a fist and pulled his arm back.

Barclay caught the blow with his crutch, slamming Duncan's arm hard. "I said FUCK OFF!"

It felt good to scream, better to hear men come running. First out of the door was Master Day, who ran the front desk, and right behind him were Tide, Lance, Bran, and two guys he didn't know. Rec was right behind them.

Duncan screamed, the sound like a really loud cornered rat. He backed up, then turned and ran, disappearing among the pedestrians on the street. Lance took off after him. Growling, Tide followed. "You wait for me, boy!"

"Fuck. Someone call Union. Right fucking now." Rec's arm came around his shoulders. "Are you okay, B?"

"Fine. I may have broken his arm." He hoped he had, actually.

"I hope you did," muttered Rec, echoing his thoughts. "Did someone call Union?"

"Yeah, I did." Tyrone was scanning the street. "I can see Tide, but not Lance or the asshole. Tide's still headed north."

"I hope Lance is going to be okay…."

Tyrone snorted. "If he didn't listen to his master, his ass is going to be blistered."

Bran nodded. "It wasn't smart running after him, either. That guy looked crazy."

"It was a brave, if stupid, thing to do," Tyrone noted. "Ah, Tide is headed back this way. I imagine he has Lance with him."

Rec pulled Barclay close, up against his body. "They need to catch that motherfucker and get his ass in jail."

"Hell yeah." Barclay grinned, though, because that bastard would know he wasn't playing around anymore. He had to be left alone.

A car pulled up in front of the gym, lights flashing, and Union jumped out. "He was here?"

"He was, but Barclay scared him off." Rec sounded so proud.

Tide and Lance came up to them. "Lance followed him until he turned off two blocks up. I think he was injured."

"I'm going to call it in." Union looked them all over, his gaze ending on Barclay. "Is everyone here okay?"

"I'm fine." He was more than fine. He felt a little exhilarated, even.

"Okay. Good. Good. I'm going to call this in and go after him." Union got back into his car and drove off.

"You ready for lunch?" He couldn't stop grinning.

"I am. And clearly you are too." Rec looked a little bemused.

"Yep. I want a burger." Lousy motherfucker, thinking he could be intimidated. No more.

"Yeah? Cool. Let's try that new WORKS burgers place. It's only a few blocks down." Rec took his hand, twining their fingers together before letting go so he could use his crutches.

"Sounds good to me."

"So you're really okay about running into him?" Rec asked as they made their way toward the restaurant, Rec walking at Barclay's pace.

"No, but I'm really okay with how I reacted to it."

"You were strong and you stood your ground. You were kind of amazing, really." Rec gave him a grin. "I heard you screaming 'fuck off.' You were pissed and letting him know it."

"Don't get me wrong, it felt great to have backup, but…." He kept moving. "It felt damn good to be able to deal."

"I bet. You've been chomping at the bit with nothing to do. You're a dealing kind of guy. One of the things I like about you."

The restaurant came into sight and they headed for it.

"Thank you. I am. I used to be, and I intend to be again." He felt like he was healing, genuinely.

"I know." Rec held the door for him. "I'm really proud of you. Like really."

"I am too. Like really. Thanks, love."

"I can't wait to get you home so we can celebrate properly." Rec winked, then turned to the hostess. "For two, please."

They got seated and settled, Rec sliding in next to him. Rec pressed close, warming him all along his side. "Mmm. You feel good, baby."

"Thank you. I do. Feel good, I mean. I was so mad, I wasn't going to let him take another thing."

"I'm glad. You have a core of strength, and I'm glad you found it." Rec's hand dropped to his thigh, sat there.

"So, did you turn in the plans?" He was ready to start.

"Uh-huh. They're putting the class up on the board tomorrow morning. We'll see how sign-ups go." Rec grinned and squeezed his leg. "I bet they go good. I bet they fill up quickly."

"I hope so. I think we could make it work."

"It's going to be great. You know all your stuff. You'll make sure I get it right." Rec opened the menu, looking through it. "Oh, I think I'm going to get the Sk8er Boy burger."

"What's that? Are you cheating on me with a burger?" He had to tease.

Rec chuckled for him, eyes bright, smile warm. "You could have one all of your own too."

"Ooh! A foursome!" He started cackling.

"That's a lot of cocks to suck," murmured Rec, barely able to keep a straight face.

"Totally. I have yours to deal with—that's enough."

"Are you saying I have a huge cock?" Rec asked, eyes twinkling, the hand on his thigh moving up and down.

"I'm saying it's a mouthful."

"And I'm saying you're making me hard." Rec glanced at his menu and around the restaurant. "We haven't even been asked what we want to drink yet. You wanna go home and eat each other for lunch?"

"Can we order in burgers for supper?"

"Yep. Look—they participate in UberEATS here. So we can even get our Sk8er Boys." Rec laughed. "Come on, before the waitress actually shows up." Rec grabbed his hand and helped him slide out of the booth.

"Don't forget my crutches."

"I'll grab 'em." Rec leaned over the booth and got them.

Barclay took advantage and seized Rec's butt, making him jump.

"B!" Rec laughed.

He went for innocent, knowing it wouldn't work, not even for a second. Rec snorted and handed over his crutches.

"That look might have worked while you were laid up in the hospital."

Their waitress came rushing over. "Oh, are you going?"

"Yep. Changed our minds." Rec put a hand on his lower back, guiding him out.

"You were great!" Barclay called back. "We're just going to get laid!"

Rec's mouth dropped open. "B!" Then he laughed, tugging him close. "Oh God, I do love you."

He winked, then started to laugh good and hard. Laughing while he crutched along made the walk seem much quicker, and Rec kept making comments, making the bright day even more so.

It was like his world was becoming lighter every second. It had been ever since he met Rec. Each moment built his confidence and helped him find his own strength.

"Penny for them," Rec said.

"What?"

"For your thoughts. Penny for your thoughts."

"Does anybody say that anymore?" he asked.

Rec shrugged. "I don't know, but I just did." Then he laughed. "Although as we don't do pennies anymore, you're going to have to take payment out in trade."

"I was thinking how happy I am. How glad I am to be with you."

"I feel the same way. All the time." Rec kissed him in front of the lobby doors, then unlocked them and ushered him in.

"Me too. I'm stupidly lucky to have you." He paused a second, then continued, "And your cock."

Rec cackled and hustled him to the elevator where he was pushed up against the wall, Rec rubbing that cock against his belly as the doors slid closed. Barclay hummed and pushed back, focusing on his need, on their desire.

His own cock was hard, and he could feel the matching heat pressing against him, Rec full-on wanting him badly. It felt so good— to want together. To be right there in it with a partner who specifically wanted him and wanted to make him feel good.

"I want you," he muttered. "Over and over. I want to be full, love."

"I'm ready to give you what you need. Plus, that plug we ordered was delivered yesterday while you were napping. I unpacked it, washed it, and set it in the drawer, ready to use."

The elevator dinged, and Rec encouraged him out, hands on his hips as he crutched his way down the hall. His mouth was dry from need, from pure desire, and he was achingly erect, his balls full.

Rec knew too, gaze traveling over his body, lingering at his middle. "You're so hot like this."

"Am I?" He knew he was getting stronger, getting healthier, coming back from his fall.

"Uh-huh. The excitement makes you shine." Rec didn't look or sound like he was teasing.

"Thank you." He owed Rec a lot, but mainly for reminding him how to find himself again.

Rec opened the door, went in ahead of him, then locked up once he was in. "Put the crutches in the corner, B. I'll get you to the bedroom."

"I can do that." He set the crutches aside and stepped close.

Rec grabbed his ass and lifted him, carrying him down the hall as he laughed and held on.

"You want the sling today, B? We're gonna take our time, and you could float through it."

"How do you need me? I'm yours. Every inch of me."

Rec set him on his feet and took his mouth, the kiss very thorough. Meanwhile, Rec slid his hands along Barclay's back, coming again and again to his ass to squeeze and pinch and stroke. "I'm going to put you in the sling so I can move you any way I want without stressing anything."

He approved. The sling was one of his favorite things—he could fly and feel.

Rec slowly moved them over to the sling, which had found a permanent home in their bedroom. They'd gotten good at getting him into the thing, and Rec didn't even have to stop kissing him to do it. Which meant that by the time he was lying back, floating, he was also breathless, his lips swollen. His cock bounced on his belly, leaving wet, soft kisses on his skin.

Rec had stripped too, and his body was beautiful, all washboard abs and defined muscles. Rec's cock was hard and glistening at the tip, and Barclay knew Rec was ready for him, wanted him. He licked his lips, hungry for anything Rec wanted to give him, to be full and stretched and taken.

"I snuck a pair of nipples clamps in with that plug order. I thought, until we got your nipples pierced, they'd be a fun addition." Rec rubbed his thumbs against Barclay's nipples, the touch firm, solid.

His breath hiccupped for a moment. Nipple clamps. He hadn't had anything done to his nipples since Duncan had pulled out his nipple ring. He should have left the fucker that day.

Rec pinched his right nipple hard. "Pay attention, baby."

"I was!" Okay, so maybe he'd been a little distracted.

"Good. I want to make sure I have your full attention when I put the clamps on."

"I do. You do. I mean, I am. Focused."

Rec chuckled. "Are you sure?" He wasn't given a chance to answer before Rec pinched both nipples together, making him arch in the sling. "God, you look good."

His legs tensed, relaxed, then tensed again as Rec pinched and tugged rhythmically.

"It's like you're dancing," Rec noted as he continued to work Barclay's nipples. He was obsessed. Barclay couldn't complain about that.

"You make me need to move. Your fingers drive me mad."

"You're allowed to move as much as you want," Rec told him, a little grin playing at the corners of his lips.

When Rec had his right nipple dark red and aching, he placed the nipple clamp on it and slowly let the teeth close over Barclay's nipple.

Barclay gasped, a flame lit on his skin for a second. He breathed deeply, even as Rec crooned for him to do so. Then Rec flicked the clamp, and that flame lit him up again.

"Rec. Rec, take it off." Except he didn't know whether he wanted that.

"That wouldn't be much fun. And I've got the other one to put on still." Rec flicked the nipple clamp again, then began to play with his scarred nipple, drawing it up until it was nice and hard.

"But…." His eyes crossed, and he gulped in air, his cock achingly hard.

"I'll get to your butt eventually, I promise." Rec cupped one asscheek and squeezed, and then he placed the second nipple clamp on. Barclay's chest burned from his nipples outward.

He wanted to scream. To shout and buck and curse. All that came out was a moan, his toes and fingers curling hard.

"I have you, B. Breathe. I have you."

He nodded. He knew that. He believed it.

Rec smiled down at him. "I'll always give you what you need."

He knew that too.

Rec flicked the nipple clamps—both of them at the same time—making him buck up despite the sling.

"That's good, hmm?"

"It's big." He wasn't sure if it was good.

"Big is good." Rec rubbed his belly, the contrast with the burn of the clamps on his nipples just about perfect.

He began to relax, to breathe in and out, nice and steady.

"That's it, B. You're doing great." Rec flicked the clamps, then rubbed, then flicked, then rubbed, over and over. It was intoxicating as fuck.

He began to moan, the sounds filling the air. He knew Rec didn't mind his sounds.

"That's it—show me how much you like it." Rec kissed his throat, then each of his nipples. His belly, the tip of his achingly hard cock. His balls before the balls of his feet. "Love your body. Every damn inch."

It wasn't just words either. Rec proved it, lovingly touching every inch of him. Gentle, firm, light and easy, more intense—Rec gave it all to him. He felt cherished and turned on at the same time. A buzz moved through him, and he twisted his hands in the straps.

"I'm getting to you," murmured Rec, speaking the words against his skin and leaving it tingling and eager for touches.

Rec licked each of his nipples, barely touching the clamps, making it almost gentle, like a whisper. Then Rec blew, the air shocking and cold against his heated nips.

He cried out, and Rec blew again. This time it was less shocking and more enjoyable, the cool air spreading a new feeling along his heated skin. He undulated, the sling moving with him, swinging him in the air.

"Hungry man, dancing for me, needing me."

He didn't have any reply for that; it was all true. He kept undulating, kept moving as much as the sling would let him. Rec continued to touch, to worship his body with warm, eager fingers.

Soon, though, he needed more—more pressure, more pleasure. More Rec. Like he knew—he always knew—Rec moved to his cock, fingers playing across the head.

"I picked up another toy along with the plug and the clamps. Do you want to hear about it?"

He nodded. Of course he wanted to hear about it.

"It's called a penis plug, and well, you can imagine what it does from the name. It's a little plug that goes into your slit. It keeps your come inside you when you orgasm. It's going to be glorious."

"What? You're serious? It stays in?"

"It does. For as long as we want. You're going to love being plugged from both ends." Rec touched one thumb to his slit, the other to his hole, and pressed against both at the same time. All Barclay could do was gasp and buck, hips rolling. He pushed up, then back, then up again.

"Mmm, yeah. I knew you'd love this. Knew you'd get off on being filled cock and ass, being fucked in both too. You're such a sensualist." Rec kept working with him, adding pressure as he rocked.

"I don't know about both, but I'll try."

"We'll do the penis plug first because it's the one that's new. And I'll fuck you before I plug your ass."

"I...." How weird could it be? He'd fallen four stories, he'd survived that, so he could do this.

"Should I just do it?" Rec asked, pressing his thumb right into Barclay's ass. The burn echoed the one in his nipples. "Or do you want me to keep talking about it so you can imagine what it's going to be like?"

"More. More. Please." That thumb wasn't enough.

"Your cock slit first. Or should I fill your ass with a little plug to grip while I fill your slit…." Rec tilted his head. "Mmm, yeah. I think that's the way to go."

He grabbed the lube and slicked his fingers up. Barclay found his toes curling again, this time with anticipation. He loved being filled, loved to feel Rec prepping him first. All of it. Rec drove him out of his mind. "Love when you touch me inside."

"Yeah, there's very little I like doing more." Rec rubbed his hole with a slick finger, then pressed it into him, smooth and easy. "Oh yeah. Love your heat and the silk of you inside."

He could soar, fly higher and higher, just with that touch.

Rec pushed his finger deeper, slowly fucking him with that little digit. He knew more was coming, and he was able to go with it, float there and let Rec push him higher.

He lost himself in the sensation, barely noting when one finger became two. It just sort of happened, his ass suddenly fuller. He loved the stretch, that slight burn that faded into the most amazing ache. But most of all, he loved the sensation of being filled.

Rec's fingers touched his gland, the lightning shooting from that point to his clamped nipples, lighting both up. Several more bumps had his cock bouncing on his belly, leaving fat drops of precome on his skin.

"Jesus!" He pushed down, riding that touch faster, rocking down as best he could.

"I love it when you take what you want." Rec gave him another finger, this stretch more of what he was craving. "Gonna put that pretty little plug inside you. Keep you stretched and filled so that when I'm finished putting the penis plug inside your cock, I'll be able to take the butt plug out and sink into you straight away."

Rec always made the most wonderful plans and told him all about them, making him so damn hot. Rec always followed through too, which made the anticipation that much sweeter.

He nodded. Why play hard to get? Seriously? They both knew what they wanted.

Rec pulled his fingers away, leaving Barclay empty, but he knew Rec wouldn't leave him empty for long. Sure enough, a moment later he felt the cold, blunt head of the plug pressed against his asshole. He moaned softly. It wasn't Rec, but it was a promise of what was to come.

Rec pushed it all the way in, circled it a few times, then settled it right there in the perfect spot. He moaned, shifting in the sling to feel it inside him. Leaning in, Rec pressed a kiss on his ass, then on his balls.

"My good boy, needing me."

"Always. It will be you soon."

"It will be." Rec put something on his belly. "That's the plug that's going into your cock. It'll keep you from coming. Your orgasms will be internal as long as it's in you." Rec stroked his cock several times.

"You'll take it out if I need you to." It wasn't a question.

"Of course. You'll take it, though. I know you're going to love it." Rec kissed the top of Barclay's cock, then pressed the tip of his tongue into the little slit.

"I might not. I don't know." Fuck, that was so hot.

Rec laughed. "If you don't, I'll let you do it to me." That was quite the offer.

"Why would I want to do something I didn't like to...." He arched as Rec pressed in again.

"I'm not in the least bit worried about you not liking it." Rec grabbed the lube and splurted it on top of his hole. It was surprisingly cold.

"I—Whoa." He swore he could feel his balls draw up.

Rec pushed the lube into his slit, then put more on the tip and pushed more into him. "I have to make sure you're good and slick before I put this in. And if you feel like you need more lube, let me know and I'll give you more."

"Never... never felt that before."

"I love that I can give you new sensations. It's only going to get better, I promise." Rec grabbed the metal piece that was on his belly and lubed it up liberally. "Are you ready, B? Ready to feel me slide this metal into your cock?"

"No." He'd never be ready. Never.

"It's time, though." Rec grabbed his cock and squeezed it, turning his slit into a little circle. Then he took the little plug and put the tip into Barclay's cock.

He held his breath, his whole body gone tense with anticipation.

Rec moved slowly, putting the tip inside him and moving it downward as he watched. The very tip disappeared, then more.

"Please." He squeezed his eyes shut because he couldn't watch.

"Please what?" Despite the question, Rec continued to feed the metal into him. He could feel it beginning to spread his slit wider, could feel the tip in deep. Maybe not that deep yet but deeper than anything had ever been aside from medical crap.

"I don't know."

"That's okay. This is really, really new." Rec drew the plug up out of his slit, added more lube, then began to work it in again. Then he pulled it out and pushed it back in that small amount, over and over. Fucking his slit. The burn eased, leaving behind an ache, a pressure, need.

Rec somehow knew, and the minute that happened, he began feeding the metal deeper. Now the thickest part of it pushed against the sides of his slit, bringing everything back up again—the ache exploding into fire that burned so good.

"Rec!" He arched, his body clenching hard. The plug in his ass suddenly felt bigger, better, as he squeezed down around it. There was no way for him to squeeze around the plug in his penis.

"I'm right here. I've got you. And you're good. You're so very good, I promise."

"I need more! This isn't enough!"

"More is coming." Rec fed more of the little plug into him, the widest part disappearing inside him now.

"Fuck!" He threw his head back and screamed, the sensation wild and wonderful as fuck.

"Your wish is my command." Rec began to fuck his slit, metal sliding out and back in again, and again and again. It was overwhelmingly good.

He soared, wild sounds pouring out of him in a rush. Rec moved the plug faster, fucking him with it. Everything disappeared. Everything. He was blind to everything but the amazing sensations centered in his cock and moving out from there.

"Knew you'd like it, baby." Rec sounded so smug.

He would have stuck his tongue out, but he was too busy having his mind blown.

Rec continued to fuck him with the plug, and Barclay had no idea when he was going to stop, but he didn't think it mattered—he didn't care about anything but what was going on right now. Rec. The plug. His need.

"Do you feel like you're going to have to come soon?" Rec asked, jostling the base of the plug inside his ass.

"I don't know. I hope not. I want it to go on and on."

"That's the good thing about the penis plug—it won't let you shoot so you can orgasm over and over and over." Rec stopped fucking him and instead nudged his balls, rolled them and shook them. "These won't be empty until I take out the plug."

"Please. Fuck me. Fuck me hard." He wasn't too proud.

Rec went back to fucking his cock, pushing the plug in and out. It was what he needed. How could Rec have known what he needed when he'd had no idea himself? Rec did know, though, and how wonderful was it that he was giving him exactly what he needed.

His balls throbbed, and the plug inside him was too small. "More. Fuck my ass."

"Demanding, pushy boy." Rec pulled the plug out of him. No teasing, no playing around. He just yanked it out and slammed himself in.

Barclay screamed, trying to meet the thrust, but the sling held him close. Rec wrapped his hands around Barclay's hips and found a rhythm, pounding into him, all heat and hardness. There was nothing he could do but take it, Rec fucked him, the clamps jiggling with every movement. His cock bounced against his belly, the top of the penis plug touching off his muscles.

All the sensations morphed together, twined into one magnificent pleasure. He could feel his orgasm building and building, but he couldn't come. He shook his head from side to side, gasping for each new breath.

"Please. Rec! Take it out. I need to come."

"You can orgasm without coming." Rec started into his eyes. "You can."

He shook his head again.

"You can," Rec insisted.

"I can't."

"I'll help." Rec reached up and took off one of the nipple clamps, and the sudden rush of blood into his pinched flesh made him scream, his whole body convulsing as he orgasmed.

He'd never felt anything like it. The orgasm moved through his entire body before settling back in his balls and making them throb. He was breathless and shaking when it was done.

Rec's mouth covered his, breath pushing into his lungs. He gasped loudly, pulling the air in, staring up into Rec's eyes. That gaze bore down into him, through him, and it was pure magic.

Then Rec started moving once more, and he could feel the pleasure building again. It was impossible, but it was happening.

Rec pushed harder, thrusting in and hitting his gland. He didn't want this to end. He wanted it to go on forever.

If he was very lucky, it would.

Chapter Twelve

REC PAID for the pizza they'd wound up ordering instead of burgers and brought it back to Barclay, who was reclining on the couch, looking blissed out. Which he totally should. Rec had fucked him, fucked his slit, clamped his nipples, and finally plugged him with the brand-new, much-larger-than-he'd-used-before plug, and Barclay had floated on the sling the entire time.

"How's your ass?" Rec asked, grinning.

Barclay wiggled, then gasped softly. "It's so big."

"Too big?"

Barclay pinked. "No."

He grabbed a couple slices of the pizza and handed one over to Barclay, then sat back, cuddling next to his boy and turning the movie back on. They were up to *Dr. Strange* in their Marvel movie marathon. Longest marathon ever. But then they were watching Marvel's *Agents of Shield* in between, so they followed the timeline. Barclay had teased him for being a completist. He'd admitted to being guilty as charged.

"This is the guy everyone thinks is so hot," he told Barclay of Dr. Strange. "I mean, I like the accent, but he's… I don't know, uptight?"

"I wouldn't toss him out of bed for eating crackers."

"What?" He caught on when he saw the twinkle in Barclay's eyes. "Nobody eats crackers in our bed except you and me, B."

They laughed together and he loved that, being able to share joy with this man. He reached over and took Barclay's hand, curling their fingers together. Pizza was totally one-handed food.

The phone rang as he was on his third slice, and he almost ignored it, but a quick glance at the caller ID told him it was Union. He swallowed his mouthful and accepted the call.

"Union. Hi. What's up?"

"Hey. I've got some news."

"News? Yeah?" He sat up straight, put down the rest of his pizza, and paused the movie. He put his phone on speaker. "Barclay is here with me, and I've put you on speaker."

"Hi, Barclay. Okay. We found Forsythe and were chasing him. He went up to the roofs, and we followed. He tried to jump from one roof to another and didn't make it. He died on impact."

"Oh wow." Rec took a deep breath, relief flooding through him. Barclay's ex wouldn't be stalking Barclay anymore. He wasn't going to hurt Barclay ever again. "Thanks for letting us know, Union. We really appreciate it."

"No problem. If you have any questions…."

"Are you going to need us for statements or anything?"

"It'll depend on how the investigation into his death goes. We got statements from you both when he vandalized Barclay's place. But someone will be in touch if we need anything else from either of you."

"Of course. Hopefully the investigation goes your way."

"There were lots of witnesses, and there was a warrant out for his arrest. It should be just a formality."

"Well, thanks for letting us know. And thanks for everything you've done. It meant a lot that you believed Barclay off the bat."

"That's what I'm here for. I'll see you guys around. Take care."

"You too." He hit the button to end the call and turned to Barclay. "It's over. He's dead."

"Yeah. Yeah. It doesn't seem right to be happy that he's dead."

Rec reached out and squeezed Barclay's leg. "You didn't kill him, B."

Barclay's lips twisted. "No, I know. But it's just… it feels grizzly to be happy about it."

"Then don't be happy he's dead. Be happy that the stalking is over. That he can't do anything else to you." Rec was. Rec was very happy that they didn't have to worry about Barclay's ex anymore.

He watched the emotions chase across Barclay's face. Finally, Barclay nodded. "Yeah. I am happy he's not going to be lurking around. I wanted him to leave me alone and to go to jail, but I didn't want him dead."

"No, because you're a good person. And being relieved he's out of our lives does not suddenly make you a bad person."

"You're right." Barclay put his chin up. "I told him to leave us alone. I told him to fuck off. If he had just run away and disappeared, this would never have happened."

"Yes, exactly." He squeezed Barclay's leg. "Are you okay?"

Barclay didn't hesitate to nod. "I am. I was okay this morning when I told him where to go. I'm not letting him control my life or my feelings anymore. Seeing him today…. Well, I was done with letting him have any power over me. And I knew I had friends at my back who would come running if I needed them to, and they did—you did. Life is good—I'm happy and I'm soon going to be back to my old self healthwise."

"Yeah, you're going to be running circles around me in no time. That would be an interesting sensation with that plug still in…."

"Rec!" Barclay laughed, pressing close to his side, sweet cheeks pinking up nicely.

"What? You know you love the plugs." He knew Barclay loved the plugs too. Hell, they'd picked this one out together.

"I do."

"Well, then." He took Barclay's lips, the taste of Barclay himself right there beneath the pizza. Barclay opened up for him, easy as pie, and Rec deepened the kiss.

"I love you, Reece." Barclay looked into his eyes, expression so serious.

"I love you too, B. Barclay." He grinned against Barclay's lips. He felt light and happy, easy in his skin. He hadn't realized that Forsythe still being out there had been weighing on him that much, but clearly it had been—he felt so much better now. Barclay was safe.

Grabbing the bottom of Barclay's shirt, he pulled it up to expose Barclay's belly and nipples. The sweet nips were still dark red and swollen from the clamps, and he leaned in, drawn to them. He touched one with his tongue, then blew on it.

Barclay arched for him, a soft groan filling the air. "Do it again."

Laughing, Rec did, with the other nipple this time.

"It feels so good." Barclay wrapped a hand around the back of Rec's neck. "You could keep doing that as long as you like."

"Supersensitive. I love it." Rec wrapped his lips around one hardening nub and sucked gently, then drew back to cool the heated, wet flesh down with another puff of air.

Barclay's body clenched, the half-hard flesh hidden behind his sweats quickly tenting the material out.

"Are you working the plug with your ass, B?" Rec wanted him to, so if he hadn't been, hopefully having it mentioned meant Barclay was doing it now.

Barclay pinked, though, telling Rec that he had indeed been working the thick plug. Rec smiled up at Barclay, loving the way his eyes were glazing over. He'd put that look on Barclay's face, made everything but pleasure disappear for his boy.

"You make me feel so many good things." Barclay ran his fingers through Rec's hair. "I want to make you feel good too. It's only fair you get a turn at having all the focus on you."

"How about we test out just how good of a couch this is," Rec suggested. "So we can give it a proper rating."

"We've tested it pretty thoroughly, I think. I mean, it's survived quite the pounding a time or two."

"Yeah, but we need to know if it gets a 69 or not. I think it's got enough room for us to do that, but until we've proven it…."

Barclay laughed for him, but he was nodding. "Yes. I can definitely get behind testing the couch's 69 rating."

"You don't get behind a 69—you get in front of it."

Barclay rolled his eyes, but the sweet laughter was back. He reached for Rec's sweats and began to tug them down.

He helped, jumping up to get them right off. Then he took Barclay's down and dragged them off as well. "Lie on your side against the back of the couch." As soon as Barclay had followed his instructions, Rec lay on the couch on his side too, his head at Barclay's groin, putting him just where he needed to be. His ass felt the tiniest bit vulnerable to the edge of the couch, but he otherwise fit just fine.

Barclay put an arm around him and tugged his ass in closer, mouth on his prick. Rec cried out happily and focused on the wet-tipped hardness in front of him. He licked at Barclay first, tasting Barclay's precome. God, he loved that taste.

Barclay seemed to be enjoying his flavor too, tongue working the tip like Barclay was going to draw the drops out one by one until it made Rec shoot.

Rec tried to focus on Barclay's cock, on playing around with it, on working the slit and the glans, but Barclay's mouth was so very distracting, and in the end, Rec simply wrapped his lips around Barclay's cock and sucked. Sounds came out of him—moans and gasps and whimpers—drawn out by the magic of Barclay's lips and tongue. The pleasure was concentrated on the head of his cock to start with, but the longer it went on, the more it spread through his body. When Barclay jostled his balls, the sensation radiated out from his cock to the rest of him.

He sucked harder, pulling blindly on Barclay's cock as he began to move. Rocking his hips, he fed his prick deeper into Barclay's mouth. He wasn't going to last much longer; Barclay made him feel too good.

A vibration moved through his flesh when Barclay pulled him in deep and moaned. Rec shivered and sucked even harder on Barclay's cock. Barclay also sucked harder, and Rec felt like they were merging into one being, the edges where he ended and Barclay began fading away beneath the onslaught of their mouths.

The pleasure rose ever higher, and all of a sudden, Rec came, his spunk flowing from him in several long pulses. His whole body shuddered as the sensations rushed all the way to his extremities. He managed to keep sucking the entire time.

Barclay cried out around his cock as he was hit by an aftershock, and his mouth filled with jism. He swallowed Barclay's come down, pulling it into his belly. Pulling his Barclay into himself.

Breathing heavily through his nose, he kept sucking—gentler now, an easy, lazy sucking. Barclay returned the favor. Eventually, they each let the other slip from their mouths and lay right where they were, breathing softly.

"Couch passed the test," Rec noted at some point. He thought maybe he'd dozed off for a moment or two, which meant the couch had in fact passed the test with flying colors.

Barclay giggled softly. "A 69 out of 69, eh? Perfect score."

Rec laughed too, and set a soft kiss on the tip of Barclay's cock. God, he was happy. Deep down, all-is-right-with-the-world happy.

All he needed was to get them flipped back around so he could fall asleep with Barclay in his arms. Too bad the couch didn't have some mechanism to do that for them because he was feeling totally boneless and too lazy to move.

So maybe the couch wasn't quite perfect after all. He could live with that.

Keep reading for an excerpt from

The New Boy

An Iron Eagle Gym Novel

By Sean Michael

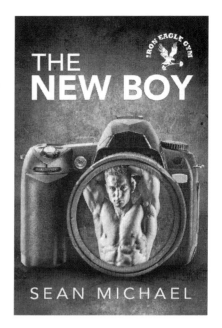

Lance Packet just got a contract to shoot an erotic BDSM deck of cards; the only problem is finding models. So far everyone he's interviewed thinks he's looking for sex for hire. Then in walk three perfect examples of men: Tide and his friends, Tyrone and Bran.

Tide Germaine is a model and a Dom. He and his best friend Tyrone opened The Iron Eagle Gym as a place for gay men in the lifestyle to work out, do scenes, and congregate with like-minded men. The modeling is just another job for Tide, but it soon turns into a grand seduction as Tide falls for the shy, self-conscious photographer. The problem is Lance doesn't believe he's in Tide's league, and he's not at all sure about the Dom and sub thing.

It's not going to be easy, but Tide's going to have to convince Lance he belongs at Tide's side as both lover and sub.

Chapter One

LANCE WAS so fucking tired of uppity assholes and psychopaths who thought "male fetish model" meant "I pay for sex."

He'd interviewed a dozen guys and they'd all been utter assholes and utterly not photogenic. He had a client willing to pay enough to cover his rent for three years for a deck of BDSM cards. A whole deck worth of images. All he needed were some hot, gorgeous guys willing to get kinky in front of the camera.

He wasn't holding out a lot of hope for this upcoming interview either. Tide. Who the fuck was called Tide? A porn star, that was who.

Lance was tempted to just cancel the fucking interview. But damn, three years' rent. Three years to build his business. Who could fucking walk away from that?

Still, he sat a few more minutes and was actually about to get up and leave when three guys walked into the coffee shop.

Oh God. They were stunning. A big black man, a small platinum-blond super-tanned twink, and the most beautiful man he'd ever fucking seen.

Oh please be here for me, he thought. *Pretty please.*

The beautiful one with the blue eyes looked over at him and smiled, headed his way. "Lance Packet?"

Oh, fucking A. Yes.

"I am." Lance stood up, held out his hand. "Pleased to meet you."

"Tide. The same. This is Tyrone and Bran."

Tide's hand was big, swallowing his up in the most amazing grip.

"Tide." Whoa. These guys were stunning and Lance was… so totally not.

Tide pulled up the chair next to him, while Tyrone pulled out the other two, making sure Bran was seated before sitting himself.

"So you're doing an erotic calendar?" Tide asked, taking the initiative.

"No. No, I'm doing a deck of cards. A fetish deck." With leather and chains and anal and…. God, he was never going to survive this. Not with these stunning men as potential models.

"Really? Oh, that sounds very interesting." Tide had an amazing voice, low and warm.

"I have a few questions. Uh. You're comfortable with that idea? Fetish, I mean. This client has very specific ideas." Lance pushed over the illustrations his client had sent.

Tide looked at them and hummed, then passed them to Tyrone and Bran.

Lance knew he was blushing, but he couldn't help it. These guys were the first ones who seemed like they might be anywhere close to workable, and they were sexy as hell.

"These are ambitious. You'll need the right people to pull them off." Tyrone sounded like he knew what he was talking about. "You need three people who are… close." Tyrone looked at Tide and grinned.

"Yes. I need men who aren't ashamed of their bodies or their arousal."

Tyrone stroked Bran's shoulder, like he was petting a big cat. "There is no shame for us in what we do. And we've worked with Tide before, giving demonstrations. Some in these exact poses."

"I'm imagining a few sessions to get all the poses and then one for reshoots. That is, if you're willing, of course." Lance couldn't believe he had possibly found exactly the men he needed. He just might get that payday after all.

"It looks like it's going to be a fascinating collection in the end," Tide noted.

Tyrone nodded, nudged Bran. "Boy?"

"It looks exciting, Master. Truly. But only if it's for art, not porn."

Master? Had Bran said Master?

"Yeah, we don't do porn." Tide shot the comment in Lance's direction.

"This is for a private collection. I'm selling him the deck, a single deck, not the original files." Those were his.

"We'd want a copy of the deck as well." Tide looked through the sketches again. "And a guarantee that any other prints would need to be approved by us."

"I can offer that. I mean, if it goes well, I mean, I'd totally be open to hiring you for more photos." Lance took a deep breath and told himself to get it together. "I mean, would you guys like a coffee?"

Tide smiled warmly. "Sure. I'd love a coffee."

Tyrone pulled out his wallet and handed Bran a twenty. "You know what we like, boy."

"I've got it," Lance insisted. "You just want a drip or what?" He was so nervous he couldn't hold it together. Professional. Totally professional. He was entirely professional.

"Don't worry about it. Bran likes feeling useful." Tyrone grabbed Bran's hair and pulled his head back for a kiss.

Lance stared, the full-on kiss shocking. *Oh God. Don't spring a woody. Don't.*

When the kiss was over, Bran got up, looking smug, and Tyrone swatted him on the ass.

"Show-off," Tide muttered.

Suddenly Lance wasn't sure if he was supposed to get Tide's coffee or not.

Tyrone chuckled, settling back in his chair and turning his attention back to Lance. "So when are you wanting to do this and how much do you pay?"

"I can pay you each two thousand dollars and I'd like to get all the pictures done in four or five days, with the option of picking up an extra day if I go through it and find I don't have enough pictures for all fifty-two cards."

Tide and Tyrone looked at each other, some sort of silent communication going on between them. Then Tide turned back to him again, smiled. "We need a contract, of course, but we're in."

"Do you mind if I take a few shots today, just to check things?" He had the contracts with him and he pushed them across the table.

Tyrone took them and started reading them over.

It was Tide who answered him. "I think doing a few shots today is a great idea. It'll let us see how you work, what we can expect."

"It doesn't have to be formal. We've got a nice sun."

"Yeah? There's a park across the street and Bran no doubt got our coffees to go."

"Okay. Cool. Let me grab another drink and I'll meet you guys in the park." Lance couldn't believe he was actually going to get to shoot these amazing studs.

"You got it."

Tyrone gathered up the contracts and stood, arm going around Bran as he got back to their table with three takeout coffee cups. "We're going to the park, boy."

"Yes, Master." Not even a question. Not a worry.

The contrast of their skin was amazing too; they complemented each other beautifully and would photograph stunningly.

"Quite the pair, aren't they?" Tide asked.

"They're striking together, yes."

Tide went with him to the counter. "So how did you come across this particular project?"

"I have a client who recommended me. We worked together in college and she thought I'd be the right choice for the job. I sent my resume and portfolio, and he loved my work." It was just like getting any other job, but with way more cock.

"You do a lot of nude males?" Tide handed the cashier a five, paying for his coffee.

"Oh. I. Thank you." How dear. "I've done some. I mostly do fine art pieces."

"You'll have to show me your portfolio." Tide sounded genuinely interested.

"Of course." Absolutely. That was totally reasonable.

Tide put his hand on Lance's lower back as they headed out of the coffee shop and it felt like he'd been hit with a live wire.

Don't spring wood. Think about mud. Bugs. Roadkill. It occurred to him that he was going to have to jack off thirty times before he shot these guys.

They joined Tyrone and Bran across the street in the park, the sunlight highlighting the way they contrasted each other.

Lance nodded. "Like I said, these are totally just quick shots. I just want to"—*have some distance between me and you gorgeous bastards*—"see what turns up."

He pulled his camera out and started shooting, not worrying about the light or much of anything. It was where he felt most comfortable anyway, and it was way easier to feel professional with the lens between him and these stunning men.

"You want us to do anything in particular?" Tide asked, seeming unconcerned about the camera.

"No. No, just hang out. No worries."

"You sure?" asked Tide. "No kissing? Posing?"

At the word kissing, Tyrone and Bran totally locked lips.

Lance let himself just shoot and not be a part of it, not think about anything but shapes and angles and light. It was so much safer back here.

"Way to make everyone else jealous," teased Tide, rolling his eyes.

Laughing, Tyrone grabbed the collar of Tide's T-shirt and pulled him into a kiss that looked like it should have smoke.

This was going to be the best fucking set of shots ever. Lance couldn't wait to see the results.

When the kiss broke, he got an amazing shot of them looking at each other, fondness in their eyes. He'd let them have that one. Obviously they were all… close.

Tide began mugging after that, doing typical model poses for him. Lance chuckled. There was something about Tide, something bright and fascinating. The man was looking at him through the lens, too. Like Tide could see right through it.

No. No way. This was his defense against the world.

Still, he felt Tide's slow, easy smile all the way to his toes. Lance sighed softly. God, that was pretty.

Tyrone and Bran sat together on the grass, talking quietly.

"So. I've got Tide's e-mail. Can you guys all let me know, after you read your contracts, if you're interested and when good times are? I have a budget for supplies, but I'll have to get with my client to see exactly what he'd be interested in."

"We have some of the things you might need," Tyrone told him. "So don't buy anything without checking first."

"Absolutely. I'm sure someone has a list." Lance knew in general what might be a BDSM prop, but he was sure his client had some specific ideas and he was in no way an expert on the topic himself.

"You don't have a list of your own? We'll supply you with one," Tyrone offered.

Lance shook his head, though. Like he had any idea what exactly they'd need. He'd put that on the client and pick up what was needed once he had that in hand. He'd been having so much trouble finding the right guys for the work, he hadn't asked for a list, feeling it would have been premature—putting the cart before the horse.

Tide took his hand. "We've got you covered."

His hand began to sweat, to tremble. "Th-thanks."

"We'll e-mail you our agreement and contracts later today," Tyrone suggested.

"Sounds good. Let me know when you're free, and we'll make arrangements."

"We sure will." Tide gave him a once-over that he could totally feel.

"I should go. I'm so glad you guys showed. So glad." Utterly freaking out, but glad.

"It was really nice to meet you. Dream of us." Tide looked at him like he was edible.

"I. What?" He lifted his camera, putting it between them and shooting a picture.

"The project," Tide said. "Dream up all the poses you want so we're all ready to go."

"Yes. Yes, of course. Have a great day. Thank you."

Looking at him through the lens, Tide brought his hand up and kissed the back of it. "Thank you."

"Oh. I. Bye. Good-bye."

He waved and ran, his cock hard as nails. Forget thirty times, he was going to have to jack off a million times before they shot anything at all.

Often referred to as "Space Cowboy" and "Gangsta of Love" while still striving for the moniker of "Maurice," SEAN MICHAEL spends his days surfing, smutting, organizing his immense gourd collection, and fantasizing about one day retiring on a small secluded island peopled entirely by horseshoe crabs. While collecting vast amounts of vintage gay pulp novels and mood rings, Sean whiles away the hours between dropping the f-bomb and pursuing the *Kama Sutra* by channeling the long-lost spirit of John Wayne and singing along with the soundtrack to *Chicago*.

A longtime writer of complicated haiku, currently Sean is attempting to learn the advanced arts of plate spinning and soap carving sex toys.

Barring any of that? He'll stick with writing his stories, thanks, and rubbing pretty bodies together to see if they spark.

Website: www.seanmichaelwrites.com
Blog: seanmichaelwrites.blogspot.ca
Facebook: www.facebook.com/SeanMichaelWrites
Twitter: @seanmichael09

THE
PERFECT
SUB

SEAN MICHAEL

Sequel to *The New Boy*
An Iron Eagle Gym Novel

While new couple Tide and Lance spend time deepening their relationship and further introducing Lance to the joys and vagaries of being a sub, established couple Tyrone and Bran discover that they still have a thing or two to learn as well.

A new job finds Bran run off his feet, and a visit to the eye doctor leads to the discovery of a brain tumor. Bran is terrified. He strives to be the perfect sub for his beautiful master and sees the tumor as a personal failing as he tries to handle every last phone call, e-mail, and text that comes in, no matter how early or late. When Tyrone finally finds out about the tumor Bran's been keeping a secret, he realizes he's been taking his sub for granted, and he works to rediscover his boy and their relationship. Of course, that's easier said than done given that Bran's job is taking up all his time and he would rather pretend the tumor just doesn't exist than actually deal with it.

It's going to take all of Tyrone's prowess as a master to help guide Bran through these troubled waters.

www.dreamspinnerpress.com

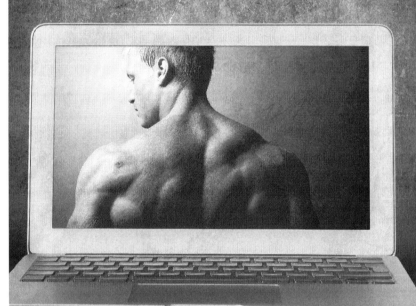

THE LUCKIEST MASTER

SEAN MICHAEL

An Iron Eagle Gym Novel

When Master Damien Richardson (Day to his friends) takes over the front desk manager job at the Iron Eagle Gym, he knows he's going to need an assistant. But finding the right person for the job is harder than he thought it would be. When he meets Saw, he thinks he's found the solution to all his problems, and maybe something more.

Sawyer Whitehead lost his master to a tragic car accident some years ago, and since then one opportunity after another has gone sour on him. Thoroughly convinced he's cursed and a jinx to everything and everyone he touches, he refuses to officially become Day's assistant because he knows that as soon as he does, something terrible will happen. He's even more determined not to get involved with Day, despite his attraction, because it would kill him to be responsible for tragedy befalling the lovely man.

Day must convince Saw that he's not cursed and that together, they can face any challenge that comes their way—in both their professional and personal partnerships.

www.dreamspinnerpress.com

THE
CLOSET
BOY

IRON EAGLE GYM

SEAN MICHAEL

An Iron Eagle Gym Novel

Way'ra Bernard is only twenty years old when his parents kick him out of the house. He has been brought up to believe being gay is wrong and he is going to go to hell for it. He tried very hard not to be gay but couldn't change the way he felt. Now he's living furtively in a closet on the third floor of the place he's working as a janitor—the Iron Eagle Gym.

Neal McPherson is an unattached Dom in his midtwenties and a member of the gym. One evening after working out, he notices Way'ra on the stairs and he's immediately attracted and intrigued, so he asks Way'ra out. Unable to come up with a reason to refuse and also interested in Neal, Way'ra accepts.

There are a lot of obstacles to the relationship they attempt to build after their date, not least of which is Way'ra's upbringing and his lingering doubts about the kinky sex Neal enjoys. But with patience and persistence, Neal might convince Way'ra not only to accept himself, but to loosen his inhibitions enough to explore and find a happy ending together.

www.dreamspinnerpress.com

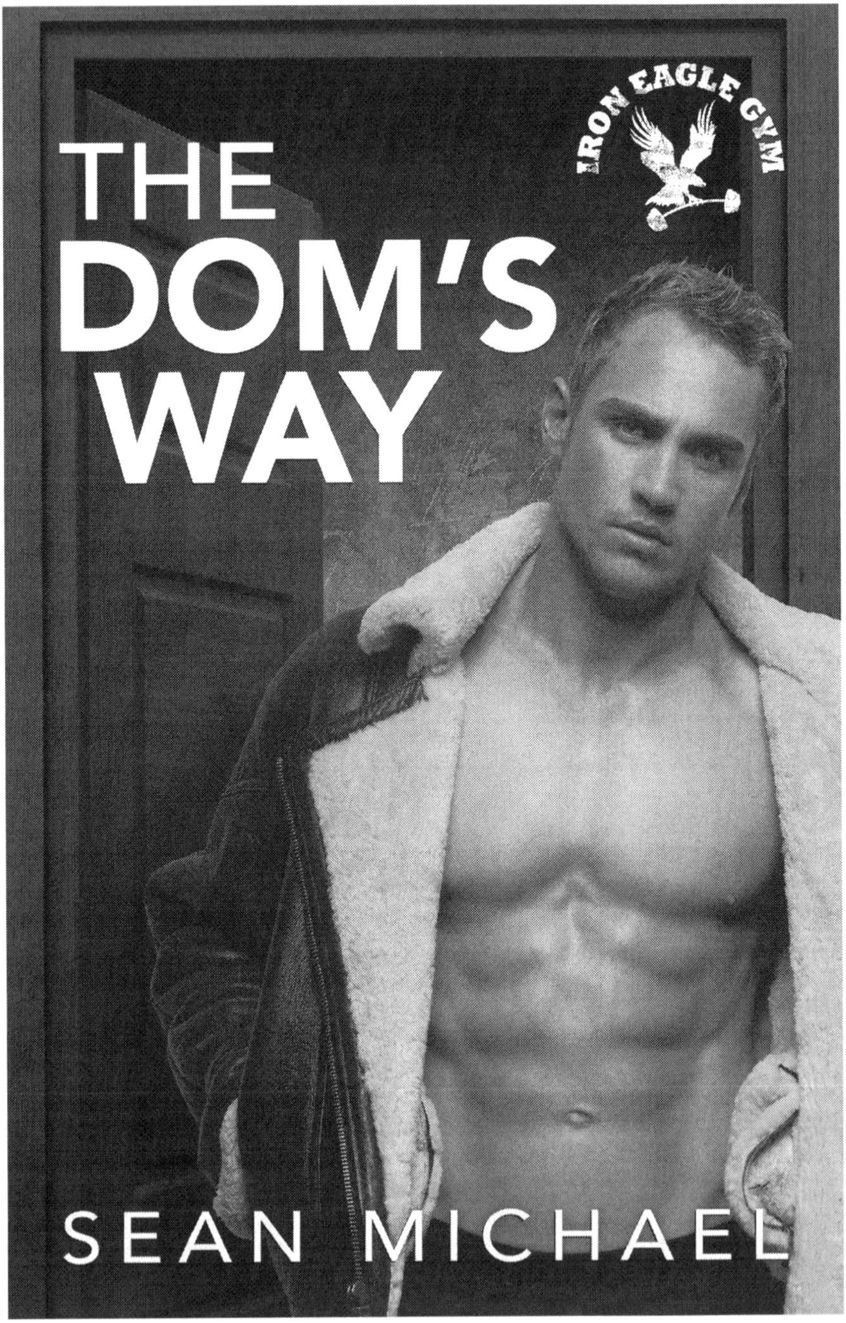
IRON EAGLE GYM
THE DOM'S WAY
SEAN MICHAEL

An Iron Eagle Gym Novel

Neal and Way from *The Closet Boy* are back, only now they're Dom and sub, and exploring their relationship through the lifestyle. Way is eager to learn everything, and more in love with his master every day. For his part, Neal can't believe how lucky he is to have found such an innocent but sensual boy.

As they learn what works best for them both, Way has trouble obeying some of the rules Neal imposes. Like the no touching himself rule. Neal wants Way to learn control, but Way, after so long holding back, has trouble not indulging. The two men must work together to find the balance that brings them each the most satisfaction and happiness.

www.dreamspinnerpress.com

THE
EAGER
BOY

IRON EAGLE GYM

SEAN MICHAEL

An Iron Eagle Gym Novel

Eight months ago Robin Secoya left his lover and master, Stack Lobond, because he didn't believe Stack really cared about him. He was sure that for Stack, any warm body would do, and Robin wasn't willing to be just a warm body anymore.

A chance meeting at the Iron Eagle Gym brings them back together, and old feelings aren't far from the surface. They decide they can't pass up a second chance at romance. But this time, it isn't just Stack's demanding career as a big-cat vet putting strain on their relationship. Robin also has a new job that takes up a lot of his time.

Will their kinky love affair crash and burn a second time, or can they find the balance that will allow the passion between them to flourish?

www.dreamspinnerpress.com